STAR WARS

LAST OF THE JEDI

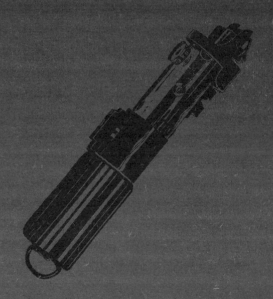

SECRET WEAPON
BY JUDE WATSON

SCHOLASTIC INC.

New York   Toronto   London   Auckland   Sydney   Mexico City   New Delhi   Hong Kong   Buenos Aires

ISBN-10: 0-439-68140-5
ISBN-13: 978-0-439-68140-7

Cover art by Drew Struzan

12 11 10 9 8 7 6 5 4 3 2 1   7 8 9 10 11 12/0

Printed in the U.S.A.
First printing, April 2007

GUIDE TO
CHARACTERS

Obi-Wan Kenobi: The great Jedi Master, now on exile on Tatooine

Ferus Olin: Former Jedi Padawan, once apprenticed to Jedi Master Siri Tachi

Solace: Formerly the Jedi Knight Fy-Tor Ana; became a bounty hunter after the Empire was established

Garen Muln: Weakened by long months of hiding after Order 66; resides on the secret asteroid base that Ferus Olin has established

A loose confederation of those who have been marked for death by the Empire who gave up their official identities and disappeared; centered on Coruscant

Dexter (Dex) Jettster: Former owner of Dex's Diner; has established a safe house in Coruscant's Orange District

Oryon: Former head of a prominent Bothan spy network during the Clone Wars; divides his time between the secret asteroid base and Dex's hideout

Keets Freely: Former award-winning investigative journalist; now hiding out in Dex's safe house

Curran Caladian: Former Senatorial aide from Svivreni; cousin to deceased Senatorial aide and friend of Obi-Wan Kenobi, Tyro Caladian. Marked for death due to his outspoken resistance to the establishment of the Empire; lives in Dex's safe house

GUIDE TO
CHARACTERS

KEEPERS OF THE BASE

Raina Quill: Renowned pilot from the planet Acherin's struggle against the Empire

Toma: Former general and commander of the resistance force on Acherin

THE ELEVEN

Resistance movement on the planet Bellassa; the group is beginning to be known throughout the Empire. First established by eleven men and women but has grown to include hundreds in the city of Ussa with more supporters planetwide

Roan Lands: One of the original Eleven; friend and partner to Ferus Olin

Dona Telamark: A supporter of the Eleven; hid Ferus Olin in her mountain retreat after his escape from an Imperial prison; now on the asteroid base

Wil: Part of the original Eleven and now its lead coordinator

Dr. Amie Antin: Loaned her medical services to the group, then joined later; now the second-in-command

GUIDE TO
CHARACTERS

Trever Flume: Ferus Olin's thirteen-year-old companion, a former street kid and black market operator on Bellassa; now an honorary member of the Bellassa Eleven and a resistance fighter

Clive Flax: Former musician and corporate spy turned double agent during the Clone Wars; friend to Ferus and Roan; escaped with Ferus from the Imperial prison world of Dontamo

Astri Oddo: Formerly Astri Oddo Divinian; divorced the politician Bog Divinian after he joined with Sano Sauro and the Confederacy for Independent Systems during the Clone Wars; now on the run, hiding from Bog; expert slicer specializing in macro-frame computer code systems

Lune Oddo Divinian: Force-adept eight-year-old son of Astri and Bog Divinian; he and his mother are hiding out on the asteroid base

CHAPTER ONE

He always heard the breathing first. The disembodied rasp of the inhalation, the echoing wash of the exhale. It never failed to spook him. He'd have the sudden urge to run, to find the tiniest hole in the galaxy and crouch in it.

Not exactly a heroic response, Ferus thought, but he was no hero. That particular unpleasant fact was becoming clearer to him by the day.

And he had a feeling that even the tiniest hole in the galaxy would be found by Darth Vader and cleaned out with Vader's usual ruthless efficiency.

Instead, Ferus Olin was here — a former Jedi, a former resistance fighter, now an Imperial agent. A double agent, of course, but if he'd known how trapped he'd feel taking on that particular role, he would have stayed back in occupied Bellassa with the stormtroopers breathing down his neck. And now here he was on an Imperial ship, some sleek, powerful prototype from the

Sienar yards. He didn't even know where he was going, because nobody had bothered to tell him. Nobody trusted him enough.

The door to the lounge hissed open.

"Staying out of sight, I see," Darth Vader said.

Ferus kept his face neutral and tried not to let his nerves jangle the energy in the room. "Just enjoying the ride."

Vader remained in the doorway, filling it with his presence, sucking the artificial light into the massive plastoid armor he wore.

Ever since Ferus had agreed to work for the Empire, he'd been an annoyance to Darth Vader. That was clear. A petty annoyance, because if he had truly challenged him, Ferus had no doubt that Lord Vader would have crushed him. So he'd gotten used to lurking beyond his vision, occasionally meeting with him, and always retreating. It was easier to stay out of sight.

There was only one flaw in this plan: Vader wasn't going along with it. On this trip, Ferus had noticed that Vader had made a point of talking to him. He even initiated conversations. It was clear that these conversations were designed to unnerve him. The Emperor had forced Vader to bring Ferus along on this trip — Ferus had no idea why — and Vader wasn't happy about it. Instead of ignoring Ferus, he'd decided to play with him, the way a felinx might bat around a field mouse before devouring him in one gulp.

In that breath mask, Vader's expressions couldn't be seen. But Ferus felt his contempt.

Ferus's blood rose. He struggled to stay calm. Vader's mere presence was bad enough; when Ferus felt his scorn, it inflamed the deep rage and the bitterness he felt.

Less than a week ago, Ferus had gambled, and he had lost. He had been certain that Vader was planning an invasion of Samaria, where Ferus had made contact with the resistance. Vader had outmaneuvered him. He'd invaded the neighboring planet of Rosha instead.

And Ferus had just sent his friend and companion, thirteen-year-old Trever, there.

Vader had taken particular pleasure in showing Ferus the smoking ruins of Rosha's capital city. They'd even flown over it before they left the two-planet system. On the HoloNet, Ferus had seen the destroyed hulk of Trever's ship. It had been blasted to pieces.

He didn't know whether Trever was dead or alive.

And the others . . . his friends. Did they make it to the secret base? Was his partner Roan Lands still there, or had he returned to Bellassa? How were Astri and Lune? Ferus had helped Astri Oddo escape Samaria with her eight-year-old son. Her ex-husband, Bog Divinian, was determined to take the boy from her. Darth Vader and the Emperor had just installed Divinian as the ruler of Samaria and Rosha.

He had no way to find out if his friends were safe.

He hadn't thought that becoming a double agent would be easy. He'd been prepared for danger and the possibility of his own death. But he hadn't prepared for the loneliness.

He was in too deep. It was too dangerous to contact his friends. He was forced to wait, hoping things would improve and he'd have some freedom to remove himself from Vader's presence.

It had been a long time since he'd felt this alone. Surrounded by Imperials, Ferus missed his own life more than ever. But that gave him something to fight for.

It was his own fault he felt so marooned. He had made so many mistakes. He had turned left when he should have turned right, gone forward when he should have remained still. He had sent off Trever instead of keeping him close.

He had been chewing on the hard pieces of his remorse for several days. Time and again he almost bailed on the double agent idea and wondered if he could jump ship at the next stop. He needed to get back to Rosha. He needed to look for Trever.

Ferus knew that Vader could pick up fear and confusion, so he tried to push back all these thoughts. It was exhausting to constantly do this, but it had to be done.

Ferus heard a muffled sound coming from Darth Vader's helmet. He knew Vader was wired into the ship's comm system. No doubt he was receiving a message.

Without another word, he turned and stalked out. In addition to being a terrifying sort of guy, Vader had no manners.

Ferus waited a moment, then followed, staying well behind. Vader turned into his private quarters. Ferus sprang back as Vader exited only a few seconds later and proceeded to a hallway near the bridge, where the pilot, an Imperial navy captain, emerged to speak to him.

Not much to see. It seemed an ordinary consultation.

Ferus was turning away when something pinged inside him, something small that he had noted unconsciously but hadn't analyzed. He was getting better at this Jedi skill — to see the tiniest detail in a picture and know when something is off.

Darth Vader's Imperial code cylinder was missing. It usually hung on his belt.

Ferus quickly made his way back to Vader's quarters. He accessed the door, which had no privacy code to lock it. Vader was probably expecting to return quickly.

The code cylinder was sitting in the dataport dock.

No doubt Vader had placed it there to update it with the new information constantly streaming through the Empire's infosphere. Each Imperial officer had one, and clearance extended upward through the ranks — the higher your rank, the higher your clearance.

Ferus had a code cylinder, too. It basically got him into the kitchen.

But Darth Vader had to have the highest clearance of all.

The possibilities thundered through Ferus's mind in the space of a moment.

If new information was being downloaded, it wouldn't have Vader's privacy lock on it yet.

The things he could learn from Vader's high clearance . . .

Any still-missing Jedi.

The fate of Trever.

Plans to crush the resistance.

Even a clue to Vader's true identity.

Ferus waved his hand over the sensor and closed Darth Vader's door.

CHAPTER TWO

Small fires flickered all over the streets of Rosha. The Empire had cut most of the power to the city to be sure it controlled the tech infrastructure. Fighting had broken out in intense battles that left more and more Roshans dead or homeless. The smoking city had lost some of its most beautiful buildings, whole neighborhoods razed by the Empire in order to stamp out rebellion and frighten the populace. The city had been pounded from the air.

Trever Flume darted through smoke and shadow underneath an eerie red sky. The taste of flight and ash was familiar to him. His own world, Bellassa, had been brutally invaded, too. At times during the last few days he'd felt he was living in his nightmares.

He had left his homeworld as a stowaway aboard Ferus Olin's escape ship. He'd been with Ferus ever since. Except for now. Now, Ferus was somewhere with the Empire. He had started out to be a double agent . . . but did he still remember his friends?

Trever thought about what had happened on Samaria. A politician had been imprisoned and killed. And the leader of a resistance cell had been arrested. Ferus had known both of the victims. Had he betrayed them?

Trever hated these suspicions. He'd thought Ferus was a hero. He'd worshipped him like a dumb, naïve kid. When really he'd been on his own for long enough to know that there was no room for heroes in this galaxy. Just beings trying to get along under the Imperial boot.

Seems like Ferus had found himself a cushy gig, traveling around on Imperial transports and hobnobbing with officers and politicians. Maybe that had gotten to him. Maybe he wanted an easier life. He'd been on the run, scrounging and hustling to find materials and support and a way to get clear. Now he was sitting pretty.

Did Ferus think he was dead? There was no doubt that he'd seen the ship burning; it had been broadcast on the HoloNet. There was no way to get word to him that he was safe.

Would he care?

Or was he one of them now?

Trever could see that Flame, his new compatriot, had her doubts about Ferus's true sympathies. She was wary of him. Her doubt had fueled the wondering in Trever's own mind. Flame had taken all the considerable wealth she'd amassed as a business leader on her homeworld of Acherin and established a fund to help resistance movements around the galaxy. She called the movement Moonstrike.

Now she appeared out of the darkness, a blaster rifle held steady. She lowered it when she recognized Trever. With a jerk of her head, she indicated the way.

He followed. He'd only known her a short time, but he'd follow her anywhere. Flame's instincts were incredible, her timing flawless, and her courage remarkable. He'd seen her pilot a plane under fire and jump out into the midst of blasterfire, dragging him along, protecting him, urging him to run when he didn't think he could make it.

Without her, he'd be dead. Another casualty of the Empire.

As she slipped into a crack of a partially demolished building, Trever followed. Inside, the building was open to the sky, but the four walls offered protection. A ramp had lost most of its surface but still led up to a second story. Blasted-out windows lined one back wall. Trever's gaze flicked over the space with an accomplished eye. As a street thief on Bellassa, he had learned to always plan more than one exit in case of trouble.

Already a small group sat waiting. Strapped to their backs or their belts were a variety of weapons. Before the Empire invaded, Rosha had been a peaceful planet, but citizens now had scavenged arms from wherever they could find them. Their clothes were stained with smoke and dirt. Some had bandages wrapped around an arm or forehead.

Here were the beginnings of the Roshan resistance.

Flame motioned for Trever to sit next to her in the tight circle.

"No names," a tall Roshan said. His four delicate antennae were tightly curled, a signal of anxiety for a Roshan. "We're going to set up a code name system after this meeting. We're all here for the same reason." He indicated Flame. "Our visitor has assured us that we can count on help from her organization."

"You need to set up an account that I can transfer credits to," Flame said.

"We need weapons and a secure comm system," another Roshan said.

"And vehicles," someone else chimed in.

"The most important thing you need is information," Flame told them. "You have to find the right insiders to bribe. If you know what the Empire is going to do before it does it, you can plan strikes and escape routes."

Trever found his mind drifting. He knew the basics now. He'd learned plenty about how to set up a resistance. He admired how Flame sat back and didn't dominate. She waited until one of the Roshans asked a question, and she asked plenty of questions on her own.

Trever's mind drifted to Ferus again. Instead of traveling with Ferus, he was here with someone he hardly knew, seeding resistance groups from planet to planet.

Maybe it made more sense than he'd thought. Saving Jedi wasn't his fight. But setting up resistance groups throughout the galaxy was more his speed. Maybe fate had stepped in and given him a push in the right direction.

Suddenly his father appeared in his mind. He tried not to think about his parents. Trever had attacked his grief long ago. He had spent months in a haze of agony and anger until he realized he just couldn't function if he continued to remember things. He had turned his face away from memory. He'd left his life behind and become a street thief.

Until he'd stowed aboard Ferus's starship and found himself reborn yet again.

What was he now? Trever, resistance fighter? Trever, Jedi saver? Neither of those fit.

Old friends in your heart, new friends by your shoulder. Was that it? Whatever the saying had been, his father had always pointed out that he should honor his commitments. Trever had to admit to himself now that he wished he'd been a bit more attentive to those life lessons. Well, sure, at the time he'd thought it was a whole lot of blah-blab, but now his conscience pricked him whenever he thought of stealing the ship from the secret base. Ferus had been furious.

The tall Roshan suddenly tensed. He held up a hand for silence.

"I think I hear —"

The rest of his sentence was blotted out when an explosion ripped off the entire back wall of the building.

Trever felt the explosion through a shudder of air that hit him like a fist, lifting him through the heavy air and slamming him down on the hard ground. A piece of rock pierced his shoulder. He tucked himself into a ball while debris rained down.

Before he could even form a coherent thought, he felt Flame's hand on his arm, already beginning to lead him. The air was full of dust and particles that choked him, and he could barely see, but she pulled him forward, both of them on their bellies, making progress on their knees and elbows while they coughed and swore, tears streaming down their faces from the smoke.

The exits he had so carefully noted were gone now, blasted into great, smoking holes in the structure. Then, when he thought things couldn't possibly get worse, stormtroopers poured through the openings.

Blasterfire streaked through the space. He heard someone shouting. He couldn't see anything. He didn't know how the others had fared. He only heard Flame panting "hurry" in his ear.

She wrenched the sleeves of her tunic over her hands — why? A moment later he got his answer.

The vent in the floor was hot, but she slid her hands underneath the smoking durasteel. As soon as he realized what she was doing, he wrapped his cloak around his fingers to help her. They heaved the heavy vent off, dropping it with a thud that was covered by the sound of cries and blasterfire.

The vent system was below, under the floor. He had looked for every exit but this one. But Flame had looked. Flame had mapped it out.

She shoved him inside, then climbed in after him. She reached out and with a tremendous heave slid the vent back into place.

There was nowhere to go. The pipe they had crawled into narrowed as it snaked underneath the floor. They crammed themselves into the tiny space and huddled together. Flame reached into her tunic and withdrew two portable breathers. She handed him one. It would help them not to cough from the smoke and give themselves away.

Directly under the floor, they could hear every word. The crunch of the stormtroopers' boots. The crackle of comlinks. A last burst of blasterfire and the muffled thud of something falling.

Some*one* falling.

"Dead." The electronic mask-voice of a stormtrooper.

"Haul that one up."

A cry and a scuffle.

"Where did the others go?"

Silence.

"Where?"

Another muffled cry.

"Kill him."

Trever put his hands over his ears like a kid, a poor scared kid. That's what he felt like.

He didn't want to hear. He didn't want to know.

Time passed. It was dark now. The noises had stopped some time ago.

Flame lightly patted his knee. "It's time."

She eased the vent off above them. She climbed out, then reached for his hand. "All clear."

His muscles were stiff, and his legs barely worked as she pulled him up and out. He collapsed on the floor next to her, then rubbed his legs and arms, trying to restore circulation.

Around them the ruins rose, blocks of stone hurled whole meters, crumbled stones, dirt, the tiled floor now pockmarked and stained. Trever looked away from the fresh stains. Hearing the battle was enough. He didn't want to keep thinking about the details.

"Some of them got away," Flame said. "But I don't think it's safe to contact the resistance again, not for a while. There was an informer. Someone who didn't get to the meeting at the last minute, I'll bet, or someone who got away."

"Who?"

She shrugged as she lifted her thick hair off her neck. "Their problem."

"We're here to help them."

Her green crystal eyes bored into him. "Trev, you've got to learn something. You have to choose your battles. I've got a bigger one to fight. I'll come back when the Roshans are more organized. I've got other places to go."

He ran his hands through his hair. His hands came back streaked with gray dust. "Where?"

"Bellassa, for a start. It's your homeworld, so you can help me. You know the Eleven."

"Well, at least nine of them," Trever tried to joke.

Flame ignored that. If she had a flaw, it was a complete lack of humor. "Bellassa's successes in forming and maintaining a resistance are starting to get known," Flame continued. "I need the Bellassans to be the anchor for the new network — an inspiration for the galaxy. What do you say?"

Home. The word rose in him, and it had weight and shape. It filled him up.

"Yes," Trever said. "But on one condition."

She frowned. "I don't do conditions."

"I need to go on my own little side trip first. I can't bring you with me."

She raised one eyebrow at him.

"But there's one thing I need help with."

"What?" she asked warily.

"I need to steal a ship."

For a moment, she looked angry. She wasn't the

type to take someone bailing out on her easily. But then she shrugged.

"Tell you what," she said. "Stealing one would be too much of a risk. There are lots of desperate Roshans here who need credits. We'll buy one."

"Hey, I could get used to this," Trever said, realizing it never hurt to have a friend with money.

CHAPTER THREE

It's not that he didn't like kids, Clive Flax reflected. He just never noticed them. They were background in the cities he visited, registering as a flash of movement in a park, or an irritating spill of juice on his trousers if he made the mistake of sitting next to one in a diner. It wasn't like he ever wanted to interact with one.

Now here he was, stuck on a constantly traveling asteroid in the middle of an atmospheric storm that turned the sky to gray to purple to navy, and he was trapped with a bunch of mates he didn't know very well. And a kid.

Lune Oddo was eight years old. At first Clive had left him to the others to watch. But he'd been eyeballing this kid for over a week now, and he had to admit he was entertaining. Opinions, questions, and a certain look in his eye, a quietness that Clive associated with his pal Ferus — was that a Force thing? You got the sense that they could hang you with your own words, so you thought twice before you said you could do something you couldn't, or boasted about something you hadn't really done.

Not that Clive himself did that. Much.

Well, whatever the quality was, it could unnerve a guy. He'd accepted Ferus because the man had saved his life on a number of occasions. Besides, Clive liked him. Despite the whole Jedi hoo-ha, Ferus sometimes just didn't have a clue, and he wasn't afraid to admit it. But this Lune . . . it was hard to remember he was just a kid.

Imagine, Clive thought, *a whole* Temple *full of these kids?* He was lucky he hadn't met Ferus until after he'd left the Jedi. All that moral rectitude would have sent him straight to the nearest cantina.

He watched the boy now as he flipped a laserball around the barren landscape. It would have been a normal-looking scene, if the kid hadn't been doing it with just his mind. Garen Muln, who was as weak as a kitten and couldn't do much, had been working with him. Garen had been some big Jedi Master back before the galaxy had been flattened by the Empire. Now he was more shadow than man.

Clive leaned back on his elbows. He'd been working since before dawn . . . not that there was dawn on this bloody rock. He was beat. Time to catch forty winks before the others arrived for the food break they always took around this time.

He started to close his eyes, but the sight of Astri Oddo exiting one of the prefab plastoid structures stopped him. He kept his eyelids half closed, pretending to be napping while he watched her shake back the springy, dark hair that could never stay confined in a cap or headband. Then she did a long stretch, hands in the air and up on her toes. She'd been working hard on the computer system here at the base. Things had fallen apart once Ferus had left, and now they were all pitching in, working on tasks that never seemed to end, working until they fell onto their sleep mats and crashed into uneasy slumber.

Astri was a puzzle. On the run from some idiot ex-husband, easy with her smiles, and quick to lend a hand . . . but with something dark and sad inside. Clive couldn't charm her, which annoyed him. After a few tries, he'd taken to watching her instead.

Astri watched Lune for a moment, smiling, then leaned down and snatched up a small rock. Suddenly, with surprising accuracy, she winged it through the air toward Clive without even looking at him. Just in time, he lifted a booted foot to deflect it before it hit him.

"Hey!" he cried.

She grinned, thrusting her hands into the pockets of her dirty coveralls. "Stop pretending to be asleep. I won't bother you."

"What do you call chucking a rock at my head?"

She came toward him and sat down next to him on the hard ground. "Saying hello."

He grunted.

"And if I were aiming at your head, I would have hit your head."

He sat up. Together, they watched Lune for a moment.

"We've been on this asteroid too long," Clive said. "It's starting to get to all of us."

"Not me," Astri said, tucking her knees up under her chin. "I'm in no hurry. I feel safe here."

He knew what she was really saying. *Lune is safe here.*

"Safe isn't all it's cracked up to be. It's no way for a boy to grow up," Clive said. "Hanging around with a scruffy bunch of outsiders."

"It's not so bad," Astri said, but she frowned.

"It's not gleaming good, either," Clive observed. "You know, the galaxy is a big place. Lots of places to hide."

"You should know."

Before he could reply, Oryon suddenly appeared behind them. Despite being a big Bothan, he had an irritatingly soft tread. Clive figured it came in handy in the spy business.

"I agree." Oryon looked very serious. On the asteroid, he had let his beard and his tangle of hair grow wild.

"I've been thinking about Lune," he said to Astri. "At this point, Coruscant might be a good option for you."

"Are you crazy?" Astri asked. "Go to the seat of the Empire?"

"They're having trouble monitoring the levels," Oryon said. "It's impossible for them to crack down completely. And Dexter Jettster has a good setup. I'm sure he'd offer you help. He could find you a place to go. Get you a new identity."

"That is, if we can ever blast off from here," Clive reminded the Bothan. Then he turned to Astri with a slight flourish of a half-bow and said, "If by any chance Ferus and Trever ever remember that we're still alive, I'd be glad to escort you and Lune to Coruscant."

Astri bristled. "I don't need an escort. I know how to get to Coruscant."

"You shouldn't be so quick to turn down help these days," Oryon advised. "We can all use it."

Suddenly Astri looked at her utility belt. A sensor flashed. "Our airspace has been invaded," she muttered.

"At last, somebody's remembered we're here," Clive said.

She began punching numbers into her datapad. "I linked the security system to a remote so that . . ." She looked up, her face white. "Lune! Come here now!" She turned to the others. "It's an Imperial ship."

Immediately, Oryon spoke into his wrist comlink. "Code red alert, weapons and front-line defense."

Solace burst out of the shelter, a blaster in her hand. "What is it?"

"Imperial ship," Oryon said.

Nobody needed to give an order. Within moments, Astri whisked Lune to his hiding place. Solace and Oryon positioned themselves behind two large boulders near the only flat area close to the camp, the place a ship would no doubt land. Clive, Astri, Roan Lands, and Dona split up into teams and flanked them. Toma and Raina remained as a last line of defense inside the first shelter. Everyone was armed with blaster rifles, alpha charges, and grenades.

Solace spoke softly into her comlink. "Everyone in position?"

They all checked in with a quick affirmative.

Clive looked up. Within moments, he saw the silver streak against the dark purple of the atmosphere. The ship wobbled crazily. They all knew how turbulent the inner atmosphere was.

The ship righted itself. It was an Imperial ship all right, a modified Sienar starship. Clive kept his finger on the trigger of his blaster. If they were lucky, the Imperials wouldn't come up fighting. The group here had worked to create an impression of an abandoned base. The idea was to lure the Imperials in and then attack.

"Hold your fire." Solace's voice was soft from the comlink speaker.

The ship executed a wobbly landing. Nothing happened for a moment. Clive couldn't see through the windscreen into the cockpit.

The ramp slid down. His finger cramped, but he didn't move it.

Then a miniature model of a Vulture droid fighter zoomed out, did a lazy twirl, and eased onto a landing on the dirt.

"Could be a trick," Oryon muttered.

A slight figure with blue hair poked his head out from behind the shell of the ship. "Don't shoot!" Trever said. "I brought presents!"

Clive leaped across the rock. He couldn't wait to wrap his hands around the kid's scrawny neck. Trever's eyes widened and he bolted. Clive chased him around the ship, but the kid was faster than a dinko.

"Hey! I came back!" Trever shouted.

"So I can kill you," Clive replied evenly.

Suddenly Solace did one of those show-offy Force-assisted leaps and landed in between them. She held up a hand. "Stop."

Clive stopped. He learned to have a healthy respect for anyone in possession of a lightsaber, even an unclipped one. He'd seen how fast those things could come out.

"Whew. Thanks, Solace," Trever said.

She turned with such vehemence that Trever backed up a step. An inflamed Solace was a scary sight. The small blue facial marking over her eyebrow deepened, and her pale blue eyes blazed in her gaunt face.

"You sneaked away. You stole a ship. You went against the group." Solace's tone was furious.

"But I was trying to save Ferus!"

"We all wanted to save Ferus," Solace said. "It was not your decision to make."

The others gathered, all forming a circle around Trever.

"I came back," he said in a faint voice. "And look at the ship! Flame bought it and let me take it, can you believe that? It's a good ship, real fast, handles like a dream —"

"You aren't a used-starship salesman," Oryon said to him. "You pledged your support to this group. That means you have to follow the rules."

"I hate rules," Trever said.

Raina crossed her arms. "You put us in danger."

"You left us here without transport," Toma said.

"I know all that," Trever said. "And I'm sorry I did it, believe me. Especially since things . . . well, they didn't work out quite the way I thought they would."

Dona held up a broad hand before anyone could speak. "Why don't we all calm down and let the boy talk. He seems to have a story to tell."

Clive backed away. He hadn't really wanted to kill Trever anyway. Just to scare him. Or maim him.

Trever sat uneasily on a stool inside the shelter. Confronting this many disapproving faces wasn't easy. As a former street thief, he was used to taking off when things became hostile. It wasn't exactly a day in the space park when you had to stay and take it.

"Things went okay at first," he said. "I mean, I crashed the ship when I landed on Samaria, but at least it was around the correct coordinates. And it was an old rust bucket anyway." He looked at them uneasily. "Anyway, that's where I met up with Flame. Of course she was in the middle of being chased by stormtroopers, but we managed to lose them. It was so totally galactic; I was up on this crystal formation thing, and she flew underneath —"

Roan dropped his head in his hands. Oryon groaned.

"You were supposed to sneak in without attracting attention," Raina said.

"Yeah, I know. Anyway, then we contacted the resistance. And I met up with Ferus. He wasn't too happy about seeing me but did agree to take Flame's message about Moonstrike to the resistance."

Solace leaned forward. "What did he think of Moonstrike?"

"Well, he thought it was a pretty good idea," Trever said. "But he didn't want to get involved. He thought it would expose the Jedi."

Solace nodded. "Exactly what I think."

Trever felt annoyed. "Yeah, I get that it's in the Jedi handbook," he said. "But you should see Flame. She's full-moon amazing."

"What happened next?" Roan asked. "Where is Ferus?"

"I'm not sure," Trever said. "He sent me and Flame to Rosha to escort the Roshan delegation. Our ship was attacked as soon as we entered Roshan airspace. Everyone else died. The last time I saw Ferus was on the HoloNet. Standing next to Darth Vader."

"So he's still a double agent," Oryon said.

"I guess so," Trever answered. Solace gave him a sharp look. "Anyway, I have to get back to Flame. I promised her I'd return the ship. We're going to Bellassa."

"We?" Solace asked.

"Bellassa?" Roan asked.

"She wants to talk to the Eleven about joining up with Moonstrike. She's ready to fund their attacks on the Empire if they're interested. Hey, Roan, you're one of the Eleven — what do you think?"

"It's worth considering," Roan said. "I'm ready to return. Dona?"

"I'm ready," she said.

"I'm more than ready," Clive said. "I'm heading to Coruscant." He looked over at Astri. She bit her lip, trying to decide.

"Lune and I will come, too," she finally said.

"I'll remain here for the time being," Oryon said. "Toma and Raina still need help."

"I'm going back to Coruscant," Solace said. Everyone looked at her. "I never agreed to the idea of a secret base," she said. "I didn't promise Ferus that I'd stay. Commitment makes me itchy."

Clive jumped up. "Well, if we're going, we've got things to arrange."

The others moved out to gather their things. Solace remained. Her eyes were on Trever, and he shifted uncomfortably.

"What is it that you're not saying?" she asked.

"After we left Samaria, Darth Vader raided the resistance cell," he said. "The leader was arrested. Not only that, the ruler of Samaria was arrested and killed. And when we entered Roshan airspace, it was like they were waiting for us. . . ."

"What are you saying, Trever?" Solace asked quietly.

"What if Ferus is one of them now?" Trever burst out. "What if he betrayed us?"

He looked down at his clasped hands. "I hate saying it. I hate even thinking it. But all those coincidences . . . I know you're going to say it's impossible."

"Nothing is impossible," Solace said in her usual blunt way. "Ferus is struggling with his Force connection. That makes him vulnerable. But . . ."

Trever waited, hanging. Solace was brusque and short-tempered. He wasn't sure how much he liked her, but he knew he depended on her. He valued her opinion. She didn't factor in prejudice or emotion.

"I trust him," she said.

The relief that filled him wasn't enough to quiet his doubts. But it felt good, all the same.

He went off to the galley section of the pod to grab some grub. It wasn't until he had eaten his fill and headed back that he saw that she was still in the same position. Still thinking.

CHAPTER FOUR

Ferus felt sweat spring out on his neck as he sat at Darth Vader's console. Updating a code cylinder took only seconds, so the dark figure could return for his at any time.

Ferus couldn't load information on his own dataport and crack it later. The files would be scrambled into complete garbage if he did. He could only flip through the files that had been downloaded in the recent updating. Most likely some of them would need passwords to actually read the contents. He'd have to see what he could glean and then commit it to memory.

He removed the code cylinder from the dock and stationed himself by the door. He'd be able to hear Vader's footsteps from here.

He set the cylinder to holo-mode and flashed through the datafiles, concentrating on those with Vader's high clearance. As a Jedi, he had been trained in information retention, but he was rusty. He tried to make the flow of information distinct in his brain and not a blur.

But Imperialization *was* a blur. Planets to be whipped into shape, rulers to intimidate, alliances to smash, a new agreement with Sienar Fleet Systems . . . but nothing helpful. Nothing he could use.

The information on Rosha didn't demand a privacy code. He flipped through it. A watch list, a raid that captured the early leader of the resistance, scientists to be put under surveillance, an accounting of government wealth. Standard stuff. Nothing about Trever.

But here. Ferus moved on to the files already on the cylinder. Vader's private files. They were under a security lock. They didn't even have titles. They were the ones he needed to see.

Ferus was an expert code breaker. He expected this code to be tough, but it was tougher than anything he'd seen. Just when he thought he'd solved it, he realized he was still left with gibberish.

He couldn't risk the time it would take to break it. Frustrated, he pounded his fist on the arm of his chair. Time was running out.

Desperately, Ferus took one last race through the codes.

He almost missed it. It would have been easy to. One title of one file was uncoded, even though the file itself was hidden behind walls of coding.

TWILIGHT.

Along with the title was a brief description. LSO. Ferus knew from his short time in the Empire that this stood for Large Scale Operation. Order 66 had been a LSO. The subheading was *Planning/Implementation/ Contacts.*

Then he heard the sound that always chilled him. But this time it stopped his heart.

Breathing.

Close. Too close. Vader was right outside the door.

Ferus's command of the Force was growing all the time. He just hated to have to rely on it.

He had no choice.

Ferus sent the code cylinder into the air as he threw himself into a chair. Using the Force, it sailed across the chamber and slid into the dock just as the door hissed open and Darth Vader walked in.

"To what do I owe this intrusion?" he asked.

"The door was open, so I made myself at home," Ferus said, lounging in the chair. "I'm getting bored. I thought I'd pop by and see if you received my orders yet."

"You are a petulant child," Vader said.

He stood silently for a moment. Had Vader seen? He didn't think so. Did he suspect something? Definitely.

"But in this case," Vader finally said, "you will get your wish. The Emperor wishes your presence in the conference room."

Vader picked up the code cylinder and slipped it into his utility belt. Ferus found he was able to breathe again. He followed Vader back down the hallway to the conference room. The door slid shut behind them and the light turned red, indicating that a secure communication would take place.

The hologram of the Emperor had a purplish cast, the color of a bruise.

"Here are your orders," the Emperor said. "You are to proceed to Bellassa."

"Bellassa?" Ferus couldn't stop from blurting out the word. Of all the places in the galaxy, he hadn't expected to be sent back to his homeworld.

"Lord Vader needs assistance," the Emperor said. "The Empire finds itself in need of Bellassan expertise. They are to shift their factories from the production of luxury goods to communications and infrastructure technologies. This will be of benefit to them as well. Their economy is stagnating, and we will offer a needed boost. We're importing scientists as well."

Their economy is in trouble because of your invasion, Ferus thought angrily. This was one of the difficult problems of being a double agent — keeping your facial expressions neutral.

"You will attend various meetings," the Emperor went on, "covered by the HoloNet and broadcast throughout Bellassa, in which the factory overhaul will be discussed. Naturally, we want to focus on the creation of jobs and new technologies."

Of course, Ferus thought. Now he understood. He was being sent to his homeworld to sell this project to his fellow Bellassans. His very presence would be used as a club to batter Bellassans into submission. He was the former resistance hero who had thrown his support to the Empire. He would be the poster boy for collaboration and surrender.

It turned his stomach. Everyone would see him. Everyone would despise him. He didn't know if he had the power to make anyone lose hope, but even the possibility of that sickened him.

But he couldn't back out. He had to do it. Now more than ever. He didn't know what Twilight was. But he knew that the Empire was planning to strike against a large, spread-out target . . . so he had to find out what the target was, and when the attack was planned.

Then he had to return to Rosha and find Trever . . . which he wouldn't be able to do if he defied the Emperor now.

Suddenly the comm unit crackled.

"I left orders not to be disturbed!" Darth Vader's voice was like a laserwhip.

"Lord Vader, we have starfighters on our radar not registered to the Bellassan government," the captain said. "Possible members of the resistance."

"I'll come up to the bridge," Vader said.

"It appears you are needed," the Emperor said. "You both have your orders."

The hologram faded. Obviously the Emperor was not concerned about the ships. He knew Lord Vader could handle it.

Curious, Ferus hurried after Vader.

Vader strode onto the bridge and went to stand behind the captain's chair.

"They haven't identified themselves," the captain reported.

"Are we in Bellassan airspace?"

"Just approaching the inner atmosphere, sir."

Ferus looked at the radar, and then out the cockpit window for a visual sighting. Suddenly the two tiny points of light moved toward them, and he saw that they were battered V-wing starfighters, left over from the Clone Wars.

"Blast them," Vader said.

"They haven't shot at us," the captain said. "They're probably just doing surveillance."

"I gave you an order, Captain," Vader said.

NO! Ferus wanted to shout. Those starfighters could well be staffed by someone he knew, some member of the Eleven.

Fire from the laser cannons streaked into the atmosphere. The first ship dived and rolled, trying to evade the locked-on firepower.

You can do it, just heel it over to starboard and push those engines . . . come on, come on . . .

The ship disappeared. Vapor.

The second ship heeled around.

"Look at him squirm!" One of the lesser officers made the comment. Vader looked over, and the officer paled.

The captain dived, the big ship moving easily, almost gracefully.

The second laser cannon sent off an energy bolt.

Pull up, pull up! Ferus felt the cry inside him.

The second ship was blasted into space dust.

Vader turned away. As he did, he spoke to the captain in a low voice. "I want that officer off this ship when we reach Bellassa and assigned to the nearest penal colony. Emotion has no place on a starship bridge."

Ferus continued to stare out into space. Had he known them, those two pilots, brave enough to risk attacking a ship belonging to the Empire? He might have. He'd known most of the members of the resistance. If he didn't know them personally, he most likely knew their friends. Their wives or husbands. Their parents.

His helplessness made his hands shake. He swallowed against the sour taste in his mouth.

Bellassa grew in his vision, and he could make out the mountain range, the forests, and then the great city of Ussa rising from the surrounding plains.

By simply traveling with the Empire, was he harming his beloved homeworld? Where did his true duty lie?

Was he about to attempt to save his world, or would he betray it?

CHAPTER FIVE

Darth Vader returned to the conference room. His Master came through immediately. Palpatine didn't even ask if the situation with the unidentified ships had been taken care of, or how. He just assumed that what needed to be done would be done. Vader appreciated that. For two beings who did not believe in trust, it was as close as they could come.

"Ferus Olin is the key to breaking the back of Bellassa," his Master continued as though there had been no interruption. "That world has proven difficult to subdue. Other systems are beginning to take note of their successes."

"The planet has become an inspiration for many resistance movements," Vader agreed. "It must be crushed."

"Your plan is a good one," the Emperor said. "We will destroy the resistance at the same time we move forward on the project. There is so much yet to be done. Years of planning. The new weapon will require more hardware, more ships, more weaponry. Governor Tarkin has coordinated the effort and will assist you."

Vader nodded. "I have assembled a team of the best scientists from around the galaxy. Those who did not want to work with us have been persuaded."

"Good. Now, let's move on. Twilight?"

"Progress has been slow, but lately there has been movement. I have complete confidence in our operative. And our eventual victory."

"Excellent."

"We are approaching Bellassa now, my Master."

"Ferus Olin . . . you must work with him. Keep him close, for just a little while longer. We can use him."

"It is dangerous to keep him close. He's not stupid. I caught him in my stateroom."

"Did he find anything?"

"Of course not, Master."

"Then why should we care? He will discover nothing of consequence."

"But after Bellassa?" Vader ventured the question. How long would this maddening protection of Ferus last? He knew there was more behind the Emperor's use of Ferus than there seemed to be. Vader was ready to get rid of him for good. Ferus was an irritant.

"I shall revisit the situation," the Emperor said.

A highly unsatisfactory answer. But Darth Vader did not question his Master.

It didn't matter anyway. He promised himself that he would find a way to get rid of Ferus Olin on Bellassa.

That would be satisfactory.

CHAPTER SIX

They had learned to choose busy space stations in tiny corners of the galaxy, where spaceliners and freighters docked. On the planet of Omman, the crush of vehicles and passengers meant that controls were difficult to maintain. The Empire had not yet completely perfected its check-in systems. Trever had no doubt that it would. Just not yet.

Their fake ID docs passed muster. They were checked through without a challenge and made their way to the smoky cantina.

Trever saw Flame sitting in a corner, her back to the wall, one foot up on a chair in front of her. He was startled by her appearance. He had left her on Rosha in stained coveralls, her dark hair filmed with dust and her skin reddened and windblown. Now she was dressed all in white, lounging elegantly at the table, her dark hair smooth and shining in a coil at the back of her head.

She was all business as she pushed a chair toward him with one booted foot. "Have a seat and introduce me to your friends."

Trever noted that Clive's gaze lingered on Flame for a long moment, puzzlement in his eyes. After Trever introduced Clive, Astri, Lune, and Roan and Dona, Clive turned to Flame.

"I think we've met before," he said.

Flame gave him a cool look. "Is that your standard line?"

"I hope I'm not that uninspired."

Solace snorted.

"I wouldn't know," Flame said. Her frosty tone told Clive that she wasn't in the mood for banter.

"Let's get down to business," Trever said. He was anxious that they all get along. One trouble with the group he traveled with was that they were all such *personalities*. He turned to Flame. "Roan is one of the founding members of the Eleven. Dona is also a member of the resistance. They'll come with us to Bellassa."

"Good. Do you have an entry point?" Flame asked. "I was thinking of landing in the mountains and taking airspeeders into Ussa."

"That used to be a route. No more," Dona said. "The Empire has patrols all through the mountains now, thick as the yarrowfew flowers in spring."

"I have a way, but it will take some tricky piloting,"

Roan said. "The Empire has shut down Ussa, but it's difficult to maintain patrols in the forested area south of the city."

"The Tanglewoods?" Flame asked. "But that's unnavigable."

"There's a way," Roan said.

"What about the rest of you?" Flame asked.

"We're going to catch a spaceliner to Coruscant," Astri said.

Clive was leaning back against the wall, holding in his hands a cup of bright blue juice that he hadn't tasted. "Any advice there? We haven't been in some time."

Flame shook her head. "Tight controls on all entry points. Your ID docs better be perfect."

"Do you have a favorite landing hangar?" Clive asked.

She shook her head. "Haven't been to Imperial City. Not even before the Clone Wars. I don't like crowded planets."

"Well, we're off," Solace said, standing. "The space-liner is boarding."

"I'll go do the preflight check with Flame," Trever said.

They all pushed back their chairs. It was the moment of parting, and no one knew what to say.

Trever was suddenly filled with foreboding. Parting with friends was so different now. He didn't know when he'd see them again. If he'd ever see them again.

"Curran Caladian told me that the Svivreni never say good-bye," Solace said gruffly. "They just say, 'The journey begins, so go.'"

Trever looked each of them in the eye, holding the gaze. "So go."

"So go, kid," Clive said.

Then Lune shouted, "So go, Trever!" making them all laugh.

Astri, Lune, Solace, and Clive headed to the departure gate. Roan and Dona went with Trever and Flame to the private vehicle departure hangar.

They boarded, and Flame automatically slid behind the controls. Roan raised an eyebrow at her.

"She's a great pilot," Trever told him. "I trust her."

Roan waved a hand. "Carry on." He settled himself behind the nav computer. "I'll plot the route."

The ship was cleared for takeoff and shot out into the atmosphere.

They didn't speak much on the way to Bellassa. What lay ahead was so uncertain and dangerous that it was hard to think about anything else.

Trever found himself wondering again about Ferus. It seemed so strange now, as if he'd substituted Flame for Ferus. Events came rushing at him like a jump into hyperspace, and he didn't have time to think anything through. It was reassuring to be with Roan, at least, someone he knew and trusted. Someone who connected him to his past.

And now he was flying right into it.

It was a long day's journey before Roan quietly announced that they were approaching Bellassan airspace. They would enter the planet's atmosphere well away from Ussa, over the wastelands on the other side of the planet. Then they would come up from the south.

Suddenly, alarms rang throughout the cabin.

"Imperial ships ringing the docking stations," Roan said crisply. "Evasive action!"

CHAPTER SEVEN

The ship went into a screaming corkscrew dive, and Trever held on. It shouldn't be this hard just to get home again. Once again, he had the sensation that the galaxy was upside down. Just as he was, at the moment.

The ship leveled out, and they all took a breath.

"Out of radar range," Roan reported. "But we're going to have to go back in again if we want to land. Usually the patrols are more random and centered around the landing platforms near Ussa. They never had large Star Destroyers lurking out here before."

Flame turned the ship and lessened the speed. "What now?"

"I've got a large freighter cleared to land at the Ussa spaceport," Roan said, monitoring air traffic. "It's got to come in from the south. If you could hug its flank, we might pass through the detection scan. Then peel off when we're close to the surface."

"Got it," Flame said.

Flame turned the ship into a quick dive, then flew in a random pattern toward the freighter. She quickly dipped the ship down, heading for the stern of the freighter.

"We're going to catch a few space disturbance waves from displacement as we get closer," she said. "So hang on."

Suddenly the ship lurched, and Flame had to pull back to avoid smashing into the freighter. As winds whipped around their craft, sending it left and right and hurling it toward the large freighter, Flame was able to keep the ship steady, only meters from the freighter's exhaust.

"The ship will blow out the exhaust soon," Roan advised.

"I'm ready. It'll be a good time to dive."

The exhaust blew, and the ship rocketed backward. Flame lost control for a split second, and the ship spun so quickly that Trever almost fell to the floor. He was beginning to feel dizzy. Flame quickly leveled out, then dived toward the surface.

"Didn't expect that to be quite so . . . aggressive," she said with a grin.

"All right, we're beyond their sensors," Roan said, watching the computer. "No sign that they've seen us. I think we made it past the checkpoint."

Flame's hands relaxed slightly on the controls.

Sunset spread out below them in streaks of hot orange and deep red. Their craft zoomed downward.

Suddenly the Tanglewoods loomed ahead. The forest was renowned on Bellassa. The towering trees shared a complex root system and grew so thickly together that their branches intertwined in fantastical shapes. There was not a sliver of space to be seen between them. The darkness was falling rapidly. Only streaks of color remained near the horizon. Flame's hands tightened on the controls.

"This is impossible," she muttered.

"It only seems so," Roan said. "Trust me. Follow the coordinates I laid out. Don't trust your eyes."

"Okay," Flame said, her voice a bit shaky, "but we're about to crash into that tree."

Trever shrank back in his seat. The massive trunk loomed ahead. Flame kept going.

The ship burst through a holographic scrim. Now ahead through the gloom they could just make out a narrow, twisting tunnel through the entwined branches of the trees.

"The resistance worked for weeks to get this set up," Roan said, leaning forward. "First we set up the hologram, then we cleared a path through the trees. The Empire hasn't discovered it yet, and we hope they never do. It's a safe pathway to Ussa."

Confident now, Flame powered down the speed and

looped through the twisting tunnel. It was now completely dark, and the trees overhead made only a whispering noise as they slipped through.

"We can leave the ship at the edge of the wood," Roan said. "It's a short hike to Ussa."

"This looks good," Flame said, easing the ship down into a clearing surrounded by a thickly tangled canopy of trees.

"No survival packs," Roan warned. "We have to look like residents of the city."

For a time they walked through the forest, which gradually thinned until they could make out twinkling lights in the distance.

Gradually they heard the hum and whoosh of air traffic, and they knew they were close. They walked parallel to the main road.

"Up ahead is the airbus stop," Roan told them. "Dona and I will bring Flame's credentials to the Eleven. We'll contact you when there's word. Are you coming with us, Trever?"

"I'll stick with Flame for now," Trever said. "I've still got my buddies in the black market. They'll hide us for sure."

Roan nodded. "Good luck. Dona and I will continue on foot."

Trever and Flame stepped out onto the road. The lights of Ussa were just a kilometer or so ahead. The airbus stop was crowded. This was where those

who lived outside the city either left their personal transports or stepped off the interplanetary liners to get to the
city airbuses. There was a small landing area crowded
with swoops and speeders. Trever and Flame joined the
short line forming to wait for the next airbus. A soft rain
began to fall.

I'm home, Trevor thought.

The airbus arrived and they boarded. No one gave
them a second look. They stood near the rear doors.
The airbus glided through the winding city streets.
Outlanders often got lost in Ussa, since it was a city
built around seven lakes, and roads were circular and
twisted around each other in dizzying arcs.

More people got on and off. The passengers began to
dwindle as the airbus reached the Moonstone District,
which was made up of warehouses and power plants for
the city. Trever nudged Flame, and they jumped off.

"Not much to see around here," Flame observed.

"We like it that way."

Trever had exited the airbus two stops away from
his destination, just to be sure the approach was safe. He
led Flame through the dark streets and down an alley. At
the alley's end, he pushed open a door to what seemed
to be an empty, abandoned warehouse. Inside, however,
there was light and activity. A makeshift city had been set
up within the warehouse's four walls. Tents had been
pitched, temporary structures thrown up, black market
goods catalogued and stored in durasteel bins. As Trever

walked in, all eyes turned to him. A tall, muscled man, with a heavy beard and a chest holster filled with small but deadly vibroshivs, stood up. Flame tensed.

The menacing man threw open his arms. "We thought you were dead!" he bellowed. "C'mere, you black-hearted scampweasel!"

Abashed, Trever walked through applauding thieves and claps on the back to the man, who lifted him off the ground and squeezed him in a bear hug that almost knocked every trace of breath from Trever's body.

Trever pounded on the man's shoulders to release him. "Glad to see you, too, Ptor," he choked out.

Ptor dumped him down on the floor and gave his head a pat. "I'll get a tarp for you and your friend so you can stake out a patch of floor. Plenty of food to go round, too."

Trever took the tarp that Ptor tossed him, and Flame helped him spread it on the ground. "When I first started living on the street, Ptor watched out for me," he told Flame.

"Seems like a good guy to have watching your back," she observed.

"Sure helped the transition," he agreed.

Someone had set up a large holoscreen, hanging from the ceiling. It was broadcasting Imperial Holovision. Ptor looked over and his face darkened. "Only thing we can get on Bellassa now. Still, they promised to broadcast some archives of the Galactic Games tonight. They're good for something, I guess."

Suddenly Darth Vader filled the screen. The room slowly quieted as the commentator's voice came through.

"Lord Vader has been specially appointed as the Imperial liaison to the Bellassan drive to convert all factories to productive ends. The crash of the Bellassan economy has been a personal concern of the Emperor...."

Darth Vader was shown standing in a room, surrounded by men and women in somber tunics.

"... gathered the best and the brightest of human scientists in the galaxy..."

"What's the matter with the rest of us?" someone called out from the back, a Dornean, a Bellassan immigrant.

"The Empire doesn't like other species," Flame muttered. "They're starting to fill all staff positions with humans."

Suddenly Trever froze. Up on the screen was Ferus. He was in Ussa.

The room fell completely silent.

"... has called upon the Bellassan hero Ferus Olin for assistance. Ferus Olin has pledged his own considerable energies to the task of retooling Bellassan factories and bringing new life to the planet's economy...."

Suddenly the room erupted in jeers and boos. Someone threw something at the screen. "Traitor!" someone shouted. The word was taken up until it made the walls shake.

Traitor! Monkey-lizard!

Ptor spit on the ground.

"I wouldn't think a group of thieves and black marketers would care so much about politics," Flame murmured.

Trevor looked around the room. "All Bellassans care about politics," he said.

He felt the contempt in the room. He looked up at Ferus again.

Betrayal. How could Ferus do this? Even as a double agent? He had been an inspiration. Now he was the worst of the worst. A traitor.

CHAPTER EIGHT

The Orange District on Coruscant had deteriorated even further. It seemed to contain more lowlifes, more menace, and more debris. It seemed more dangerous, more seedy, and more . . .

"Orange?" Clive wondered aloud. "It's been awhile since I've been here, but it was never this orange."

Solace strode a half step ahead, as she usually did, her eyes constantly moving, checking for trouble. "The Empire has left it alone, so it's just gotten worse."

"That's good for us," Astri said. She had a grip on Lune's hand. She hadn't let go since they'd left the air taxi.

"Yes and no," Solace said. "They won't let it alone for long. They can't afford to be seen as weak. And Ferus told us that their ambition is to control Coruscant all the way down to the crust. If that's their ambition, they'll follow through."

"Maybe Coruscant wasn't such a good idea," Astri said, shooting an annoyed glance at Clive. He pretended not to see it.

"No, it's the best place for now," Solace said. "Dex has a good setup. And he keeps his ear close to the ground. When it's time to move, he'll be ready. The asteroid was no place for Lune. And he's the most important thing."

Astri and Clive exchanged a surprised look. It seemed so out of character for Solace to demonstrate concern for a child. Astri hadn't even been sure that Solace remembered her son's name.

Or maybe Solace only cared about him because he was Force-adept.

Clive grinned at Astri, and she ducked her head before he saw her answering smile. She was still trying to sort out if she liked him. She certainly didn't trust him. According to Trever, Clive had been something of a con man before the Clone Wars, despite all his boasts about being an industrial spy for the good guys — whoever they were. As a slicer, Astri hadn't always been on the proper side of the law, either, but she'd been on the run from a nasty ex-husband and had her reasons.

The last thing she needed in her life was another smooth-talking charlatan. She'd made the mistake of marrying one once. Bog Divinian had swept her off her feet — straight into a life of misery. All Bog cared about was climbing the ladder to political power, and once he'd gotten a taste of success, he did anything to keep it. He prided himself on loyalty, but basically that meant that others had to be loyal to *him*. He'd failed at every business he'd tried, but he turned out to be a genius at politics. Relying on his wealthy friends, keeping grudges, paying back favors, speaking sentences with all the right words but without any real meaning, he'd succeeded past anyone's expectations. Including her own. It infuriated her that Bog had turned out to have the last laugh.

She couldn't believe what a dope she'd been to fall for him in the first place. Her father had tried to tell her, in his sweet, bumbling way, but she hadn't listened.

A longing for Didi swept over her, almost blinding her for a moment with sudden tears. Her adopted father had always run a scheme, usually behind her back. He'd been a gambler with a loose connection to the truth who'd won his business — a café — in a game of sabaac. He was an unscrupulous liar, a delightful person, and a wonderful father.

"Dex's alley. Don't make any sudden moves, they can get touchy around here," Solace warned. "We're under constant surveillance."

Astri brought Lune closer. He was as necessary to her as breath, but she had to admit that he had basically made her a coward. When she remembered the girl who had shaved her head and gone off with a Jedi, Obi-Wan Kenobi, to track a bounty hunter, she could hardly believe she was the same person. Now she never put herself in danger. She would never risk her life again. Her life was Lune's life.

The alley was narrow, the buildings around them seeming to crouch over it protectively. They had no windows, only slits, which gave them an ominous air. The alley twisted and turned, leading to dead ends. There was only one way in and one way out as far as Astri could see.

Solace stopped in front of a door that seemed indistinguishable from any of the dozens they'd passed. She stood in front of it for a moment. Then she heard a slight click, and the door slid open. They walked into a small, dark entryway. A short flight of stairs led to a closed door. Astri shivered. What if it was a trap?

Suddenly a door opened, and a column of yellow light shined down. Dexter Jettster's massive bulk filled the doorway. He rested on a large lounge with a repulsor-lift motor.

"Welcome, welcome," he boomed. "Come upstairs where you'll find friends." He powered away to make room for them to ascend.

"Good to see you again, Solace, it is," he said, nodding at her. "And Clive Flax — you may not remember, but we've met before."

"I do remember," Clive said. "I'm still digesting your sliders."

Dex chortled a laugh. "They stick to your ribs, that's for certain."

"That's one way to put it."

Dex then turned to Astri. He cocked his head to one side. Astri couldn't believe that such a massive creature could project such buoyant charm.

"And there you are, prettier than ever," he said. "I remember the day I bought the diner from your father. I heard of his passing. I'm sorrier than I can say. He was a good man. You must miss him dearly."

"I do," Astri said with a smile.

Dex chortled. "Left me a good business. I changed a few things, but everyone who came in still asked for you and Didi!"

"Thank you for taking us in," Astri said.

Dex bent over. "And this is your son."

"My name is Lune."

"And so it is, and I'm Dexter, but you can call me Dex, like everyone else does. You may not remember, but we've also met before. You were only two years old."

"I remember very well," Lune said.

"So he does, so he does!" Dex chortled. "Now. Let's get the tyke something to eat, and the rest of us will talk. There's much to say."

Within moments Lune was whisked off to the kitchen by WA-7, the antique droid who had worked for

Dex in his diner. The others went to the conference room, where Keets and Curran were waiting.

Quickly, Solace outlined where the others were, and the fact that they'd had to smuggle Astri and Lune out of Samaria. Keets and Curran listened intently.

"You can stay here as long as you like," Curran said, bobbing his head toward Astri. "It's safe for now."

"We can be on the lookout for planets where you can lie low," Dex said. "Start over again with your boy. You'll have to choose carefully. Bog Divinian has plenty of connections, now that he's the ruler of Samaria. He's been appointed the acting ruler of Rosha, too. A governor of a system now, he is. Very important."

Astri nodded.

"Now I have something to tell you," Dex said, nodding to Clive and Solace. "Something Ferus needs to know. There's a new head Inquisitor, name of Hydra. He's taken over from Malorum — he was his assistant. It looks like he might have the same interests as Malorum. He's investigating a human male with unusual powers who keeps popping up and disappearing."

"Unusual powers?" Solace asked.

"He's been seen in key areas in the Galactic Empire. Made some trouble for the Empire, I guess, and they want him bad. We don't know why, exactly. Thing is, these 'special powers' sound a lot like using the Force to me. I thought you should know that."

"Our contact is trying to find out more information," Keets reported. "But everyone likes to keep their heads down, these days. Things are locked down tight. I'm sorry to say that Curran and I worked every connection we have and came up dry."

"So let's stick with what we know," Dex said. "Word is that the order came down from high above — maybe even as high as Vader — to trap this fellow and bring him in for questioning. The last sighting was right here on Coruscant."

"Do you think he's a Jedi?" Solace asked.

"I think he could be," Dex said. "Ferus ought to know."

Solace frowned. "He's in deep cover right now. We can't get the information to him. I'm going to have to check it out myself."

"I'll give you a hand," Clive said. "I owe Ferus a favor. More than one, actually, but don't tell him I said that."

Astri hesitated. She had vowed to herself to lay low here on Coruscant. She couldn't risk exposure. She had to protect her son.

But Ferus had saved her life, and Lune's. He would do it again and again if he had to.

It was time to find her courage.

"I'll help," Astri said. "You might need a good slicer."

Dex tilted his head at her. "You came here for a place to hide, not to get involved in this."

"Ferus needs help. He saved my boy's life. And I've always been ready to help the Jedi."

"I still have some contacts," Clive said. "If yours have run dry," he continued with a nod to Keets and Curran, "I might be able to dig something up."

Solace nodded. "I still can work some angles."

"What about us?" Keets asked. "There must be something Curran and I can do."

Dex's eyes twinkled. "Oh, I have the perfect job for the two of you," he said.

CHAPTER NINE

It felt good to Roan to get his boots back on his homeworld. No matter what, he was home.

Roan told himself this, but he knew he was just searching for something — just one thing — to make himself feel better. All around him he sensed Bellassa crumbling. His beloved city of Ussa — the city that had come through a war and an occupation and still found the will to resist down to the last citizen — had now fallen to its knees. He could feel it. "As goes Ussa, so goes Bellassa" was a saying on his homeworld. Everyone had looked to the capital city for trends, for signs, for direction, for courage.

And it was dying.

He felt displaced. It was almost a physical sensation, as if the gravity on the planet had changed. Or as if the thin air of the mountains had seeped down to the plains where Ussa was cradled, invading the city slowly until every citizen felt a little dizzy, a little short of breath.

Could he be losing his nerve?

He wished he could see Ferus again. His partnership with Ferus grounded him. Ferus was playing a dangerous game now, and for the first time Roan truly feared for the future.

He walked with Dona through the familiar streets of his old neighborhood. They had been to three diners already, searching for something to eat. Supplies were low. There was water flavored with the annisa herb from the mountains. But there was no tea. There was root paste but no fruit. Finally they found a kind Ussan who had set up a stand near the park with dried fruit and flatbread. She was almost sold out but gave them the last of what she had.

Dona looked somber as they ate their meager meal. "When people get hungry, resistance can fade," she said.

"With winter coming, how long can the Ussans hold out?" Roan wondered aloud. "If they agree to recognize the governor and obey the laws of the Empire, the Imperial army will lift the blockade."

"Soon mothers will see their children crying," Dona said. "Do we really want to sacrifice our children?"

The Empire had strangled the port, strictly regulating what came in and out. It had closed the theatres and museums and entertainment complexes that had given the city such vibrant life. It had filled the green parks with its black garrisons. It had taken away all the things that made life worth living. Except life itself.

Dona brushed the crumbs from the rough linen tunic she wore. "I'm not going back to the mountains," she told Roan.

He was surprised, but he didn't show it. For Dona, the mountains were sacred, the only place she felt at home. "Why?" he asked.

"I'm staying here to help the Eleven," Dona said. "Not by offering sanctuary now and again, or a guide if they need one. But real help."

"You do help," he said. "You're our contact in the mountain area, and that's become more important than ever."

Dona turned to him impatiently. "You have other agents in the mountains, good ones, and you know it. I'm an old woman, is that it? You think I can't be helpful?"

Roan laughed. "I don't think of you as an old woman, Dona. I know you'll be helpful. I just . . ."

"Want to protect me?"

"Yes," he admitted.

"Well, you've done enough. You and Ferus. I owe you both my life, and I owe my homeworld. Here's the thing you might not realize: No one looks at an old woman. I can do more for you than you know."

"All right," Roan said. "We're honored that you'll stay."

She inclined her head.

He put a hand on her shoulder. "I just don't want to lose you."

"You and me, we're too tough for them to catch," Dona said with a smile.

Truth be told, he was glad. Dona was a link to Ferus. Before the Clone Wars, they had visited her in the mountains and stayed in her cabin. It was among their happiest times.

Roan had grown up in Ussa in a large extended family. He was used to noise and movement and laughter. His parents still lived in Ussa, but he rarely saw them, afraid he would endanger them. Two of his brothers had emigrated to other planets, and his sister had been killed in the Clone Wars, but his relatives — cousins and aunts and uncles and grandparents — were still sprinkled around the city. He could walk down any street in Ussa and it would spark a memory, usually something that would make him smile.

"I saw Ferus on the HoloNet last night," Dona said. "He is acting the part of the traitor very well. Too well."

"Do you think he's gone over to the Empire?" Roan asked. He didn't think he could bear it if Dona thought that.

"No, of course not. But I'm worried that whatever good he thinks he will do will be canceled out by the bad. He was a symbol of hope to the people of Ussa. He escaped from two Imperial prisons. He got away. Now it appears that he's bowed down to power. It looks like he's given up, so why shouldn't they?"

"Come on, let's walk." Roan stood. It wasn't safe to linger too long anywhere now. "You may be right. And if I know Ferus, he's thinking the same thing. There has to be a reason that he's remaining."

"You're probably right."

"I wish I could talk to him."

"The people of Ussa are ready to give in," Dona said. "Even in our short time here, I've heard the rumblings. If the Empire takes over the factories and builds more, there will be plenty of new jobs. People want to feed their families."

"That's what they're counting on."

"Yes, well, you can't eat integrity. Only bread."

They were silent as they walked, taking a roundabout route now, alert for Imperial spies. When Roan was certain they weren't being followed, he went to a nondescript house on a narrow street. As he and Dona walked up to the entry, the door opened. They slipped inside.

"Roan!" Amie Antin stepped forward and embraced him. "We didn't know what happened to you — when you contacted us, we were so happy." She turned to embrace Dona, who looked a bit startled at the gesture. She didn't know Amie that well.

Amie dabbed at her dark eyes. "Silly, I know. It's just that . . . we've had our losses lately. Terris and Naima."

Roan felt the sadness grip him. "What happened?"

"They were blasted by an Imperial ship. We think Darth Vader was aboard." She bit her lip. "And Ferus was, too."

There was an awkward pause. Roan knew how much it must have agonized Ferus to be aboard a ship that fired on those he'd fought beside and trusted. He hoped Ferus hadn't known that the ships had been piloted by friends.

"Amie? Bring them inside," a voice called.

Roan strode in. Wil sat on a low couch, his foot resting on a stool. It was strange to see strong, muscled Wil sitting down. He was usually full of energy.

"What happened?"

"Just some blasterfire." Wil waved a hand. "Amie says I'll live."

Roan looked at Amie for confirmation, and she nodded, telling him that Wil would be all right. Roan picked up a tenderness between them. He sensed something had changed. At last Wil had probably told Amie how he felt about her.

"I was down by the garrison," Wil explained. "Under cover, of course. We like to monitor the comings and goings. Pick up a surprising amount of information that way. I was challenged by a sentry, and I decided to run for it."

"I guess you didn't run fast enough," Roan said, taking a seat next to Wil. "Dona wants to join us. Officially, I mean."

"We're happy to hear it," Wil said. "You'll be a valuable addition to the Eleven, Dona." He grimaced. "Such as we are."

"She'll need new ID docs," Roan said. "I will, too. I can fabricate them. What shape is the equipment in? I know you had to move headquarters."

"We're set up here for ID fabrication," Wil said. "But we're talking about moving again. We've reached the point where we think it's best to move every few weeks. We've scattered the group, and we all keep moving. The only trouble is . . ." Wil hesitated. "A few months ago, we had no problem getting Ussans to volunteer their help. Even if they weren't part of the Eleven, they loaned us equipment. Apartments. Garages to store things. Safe houses. But that help has slowed to a trickle."

"They're growing tired of sacrifice," Amie said. "And who can blame them? Our successes have boiled down to simply surviving. There seems no end in sight. The Empire just keeps consolidating. Growing stronger. More organized."

"We can't give up," Roan said.

"Of course not," Wil agreed. "We need to have a success. Something big. Something that will give them hope. But we're running out of options. Our funds are very low. We need credits for bribes, for equipment."

"We might be able to help you there," Roan said, with a glance at Dona. "Do you remember Trever Flume?"

"Of course," Amie said. "We just saw him a few weeks ago."

"Trever has been the main contact to a resistance worker named Flame. We don't know her real name. She's from Acherin. She has an enormous fortune at her disposal. Her idea is to fund as many resistance groups as she can, then link them into one central operation. She's going planet to planet to contact the resistance on each one. She's calling the operation by the code name Moonstrike."

"It's an idea," Wil said, considering it. "It could expose us too much. But then again there's strength in numbers. We've often wished we could coordinate with other planets. Share information."

"It's worth a meeting," Amie said. "Would Flame come here?"

"She's already on Bellassa, waiting for our signal," Roan said. "She would be willing to fund an operation for the Eleven."

"Let's have a meeting, then," Wil said, with a glance at Amie.

"What about Ferus?" Roan asked.

Amie looked down at her lap. Wil studied his wounded foot.

"Be honest," Roan said.

"We support whatever he's doing," Wil said. "It's not that."

"But does he have to be so visible?" Amie burst out. "He's all over the HoloNet."

"They planned it that way, I'm sure," Roan said. "Ferus is stuck. He has to keep his position."

"But why?" Amie asked. "Has he brought back any information we can use?"

Roan shook his head. He couldn't explain to Amie and Wil that Ferus had a larger goal now. Ferus was looking for Jedi. He was lending his support and expertise to the resistance when he could, but it wasn't his first priority. As a double agent, he was in a perfect position to eventually access any records the Empire would have on suspected Jedi activity. Roan knew well that Ferus couldn't give that up. Not yet.

"At this point, we're wondering if the danger he's putting himself in is worth it," Wil said. "I don't believe that he's on the side of the Empire, but many Bellassans do. The evidence is in front of their faces."

"It had better be worth it," Amie said.

"I'm sure it will be," Roan said. "I'm sure Ferus is painfully aware of the image he's projecting." Roan thought a moment. "In any case, we should make contact with him while he's here. This factory business — what's really going on? It's never really what they say it is."

"And it's rarely to our benefit," Wil added.

"I'll contact him," Roan said.

"But how? He's surrounded by the Empire. He's practically attached to Darth Vader's hip," Amie said with a grimace.

"I have a way," Roan promised.

CHAPTER TEN

Attachment. Ferus wasn't supposed to have any. If he wanted to be a true Jedi, that is.

But what did that mean, attachment? Even as a Padawan it had puzzled him. He had been attached to Siri, his Master. She'd been a mentor, a big sister, a presence in his life that had protected him and, in her own way, cherished him.

What does that mean, to not be attached?

He'd asked her the question on a long run to the Outer Rim. Siri had been in one of her favorite positions, on the cockpit floor. She used to like to stretch out there with the hum of the engines under her back, her booted feet crossed on the copilot seat.

It seems so hard, Master. To have so many beings who are important to me but not to be attached to them. I don't understand what is meant by "no attachment."

Siri didn't sit up, but he saw her boot swing back

and forth, back and forth, as she considered the question. Thinking back now, Ferus wondered at the expression on her face. There had been a play of emotion that made her look soft, then sad, and then that emotion just . . . went away, and what was left was simply contemplation, a Master trying to arrive at the right answer for a question that had no answer.

It's not so hard to explain, Siri had answered finally. *To love without wanting to possess or influence. To cherish without keeping. To have without holding.*

Ferus remembered nodding. He had thought he'd gotten it. As usual, he had wanted to please her.

I understand, Master.

Siri had looked at him then and smiled. *No, you don't. It's not something to understand. It's something to strive for.*

But here he was on Bellassa, and everything here reminded him of attachment. Attachment to a homeworld, attachment to Roan, attachment to friends. He kept bumping into memories wherever he looked.

He saw that the Jedi were right. It was interfering with his Force connection. It was interfering with his concentration. All he wanted to do was slip away and find Roan, relax into the camaraderie of the Eleven.

After what had happened with the Empire, Obi-Wan had told him that because so much had changed, perhaps the rules of the Jedi would change — if there were any Jedi alive to change them. Perhaps attachment would be valued. They were up against a system that valued nothing, least of all attachment. So maybe they needed to hold what they could.

He didn't want to let them go. He didn't want to let any of it go. Any of the attachment in his heart.

He would have to find a way to make it all fit. His connection to the Force, and his connection to the Living Force. Not the abstract, but the particular. A particular face that brought him joy. A familiar walk he searched for among the throngs in Ussa. He could find strength in that, not weakness.

He hadn't known how to be close to someone when he left the Temple. He had learned. Roan had shown him how. Roan had grown up in an extended family that was full of arguments and laughter and family lunches that went on through dinner and into the midnight hour. They had accepted Ferus without question, and they had become his family, too.

And now he was betraying them. They were seeing him on the HoloNet. They were wondering how he could have betrayed them in such a way.

He hadn't been alone since he'd arrived. Vader had made sure of that. He'd been dragged to meeting after meeting, shown off like a trained animal. Constantly managed, constantly escorted, so that he was unable to talk to a Bellassan directly.

He could get away. He just wasn't sure if he should. Let them do their work, let them present him as a traitor to the Bellassans. Until he knew for sure what he was doing and where he was going, he would continue to feel the agony of this and do nothing except wait — and hope he would discover more about Twilight and more about what the Empire was actually doing on Bellassa. Because he knew something for sure: Something was up. Which wasn't very much to know, but he had hopes.

The meeting was with engineers and scientists from many planets around the galaxy, all volunteering their time to retool Ussan factories and get their economy going again.

Or at least that was the spin.

Ferus waited in an adjoining room. He was never in the meetings where the real words were said. They trotted him out for the benefit of journalists and native Bellassans. He was present for the meeting in which platitudes were exchanged and promises made that had nothing to do with the real issues.

He was in a factory. The factories in Ussa were models of cleanliness and order. They were confined to one district, and mixed both advanced technology and good design. Ussans were proud of their textiles and ceramics, which were coveted around the galaxy. The factories weren't large, but there were many of them, and they usually employed a sizable population in Ussa.

They'd been closed for six months.

Ferus looked out the window at a garden that was set up with tables and chairs for the workers to eat outdoors in good weather. Bellassa was blessed with flowering bushes that bloomed throughout the year. To his surprise the garden showed evidence of care. The path borders were sharp, the bushes trimmed and thriving. But the factory had been closed.

"I keep it up."

Ferus turned at the sound of the voice. A man of middle years, with silver hair, looked out the window at the garden. "It was never my job. I was in charge of security. Then I became the caretaker when it closed. But I couldn't stand to see the weeds choking it. It was always a pretty spot. So I made sure it stayed that way, hoping the factory would reopen soon."

"It looks like it will," Ferus said.

"Say, aren't you supposed to be in that meeting there?"

Ferus realized that the man hadn't recognized him. Since Ferus wore the clothes of an outlander, the man assumed that he was one of the scientists.

"Yes, but they locked the door," Ferus said.

The man held up a key card. "I can open it, so you can sneak in the back." He winked. "No sense riling up the Empire. Not these days."

"I appreciate it," Ferus said. Maybe he could learn something, finally, if he entered before he was supposed to.

He followed the man down the hallway and they stopped in front of the unmarked door. The man swiped his key card and the door slid open noiselessly. Ferus slipped inside. He was behind a group of Imperial security officers, all of them high-ranking. They did not turn. Darth Vader was present, requiring their attention. The gray-faced Moff Tarkin was speaking.

". . . will have the technical resources of the Empire to assist you," he was saying. "If you need assistants or additional computers or resource materials, you can requisition them. On Bellassa the focus will be on new technologies for power conduits and modular components for artificial atmospheres on an unprecedented scale. You will divide into focus groups and attack problems with new solutions. We expect innovation and we demand results. You have the honor of working on a project that will benefit the security and stability of the entire galaxy."

One of the scientists spoke up, a serious-looking woman in a dark burgundy tunic. "But what is the project?"

"That is on a need-to-know basis," Tarkin said.

"How can we work on this if we don't know the big picture?" someone else asked.

Ferus felt the power of Vader's anger ripple across the room.

"You've received your instructions," Tarkin said. "I hope that all of you are happy with the arrangements the Empire made for your families."

It was as though all the air had been sucked out of the room. The looks of impatience and condescension on the scientist's faces changed to fear. Ferus could smell it.

He realized what it meant. The Empire had taken their families. They were holding them hostage to ensure the scientists' cooperation.

The woman in the burgundy tunic spoke up. Her voice was pitched low and did not tremble. "Will we be allowed to contact them?"

"Visits will be arranged. As long as you are able to focus on your work. You'll submit regular reports of your progress to me."

When no one objected, Tarkin continued. "All of this is being done to facilitate new strides in research and discovery. You are privileged to be in a position to assist the Empire." He nodded toward the back of the room. "Bring in the press."

This was Ferus's cue. He stepped behind a pillar and waited until the press obediently streamed in, then trailed behind them. He knew what was expected of him. He was present in order to convince them that knuckling under to the Empire was inevitable, even for so-called resistance heroes. He went and sat next to Darth Vader. He watched as Tarkin continued as the official spokesperson, touting the group as a think tank called the Bellassan Project, which would hurtle Bellassa into the future with advanced technological discoveries, all of which would benefit the planet. The scientists had agreed to take up residence on Bellassa for an unspecified period, out of their great desire to join this ambitious and unparalleled voyage into research and discovery.

Blah-blab, Ferus thought. It was an expression of Trever's.

"As you can see, the great Bellassan hero Ferus Olin is here to facilitate the transition," Tarkin continued.

Ferus fought against the revulsion that rose in him. He saw the floating HoloNet news camera trained on his face. He made himself think of nothing so that his face would look blank. He did not want to give the impression that he was pleased, nor did he want to give Vader grounds to complain about him.

He had to play the game. Now, in addition to Twilight, he had to find out the Empire's real plans for Bellassa. Were the two things linked? What was the top-secret project the scientists had been recruited for?

Ferus climbed into the Imperial airspeeder with the rest of the security crew. They sped through the streets of Ussa back to the Bluestone Lake District at the center of the city. The garrison, a blight on the landscape, rose from the former Commons. Once the Commons had been green parkland that rolled for kilometers, a central place for Ussans to gather.

"Hangar's full," the pilot said. "You'll have to walk from here."

Ferus got out with the others. He'd walked across this green thousands of times in what felt like a former life. He started down the slate walkway to the garrison. The others fell into step around him in what he knew was a flanking maneuver to keep him from turning off.

Ahead he saw a splotch of paint on the sidewalk, as though someone had been walking with a dripping can. Ferus counted to twenty-five and saw another red splotch. Then another twenty-five. A yellow one.

Impatiently, the officers hurried ahead. He was left with the stormtroopers. No doubt they had their orders to surround him. He felt the shoulder of the guard next to him brush his own. His footsteps matched theirs. They were subtly guiding him toward the garrison entrance just a few meters away.

But the marks told him he had to ditch them somehow. It was a code so ingrained in him it was like a voice in his ear.

Roan needed to see him.

CHAPTER ELEVEN

Bog Divinian bounced on the chair in his new office on Rosha. It was a silly indulgence he allowed himself when no one was around. He couldn't believe he was actually here, a ruler of a whole system. Of course Samaria was only a two-planet system, but it was in the Core, and it was a start.

He looked out the window and down on the ruins of the city. The smoke was still thick over the buildings. He had already drawn up plans to rebuild the city. Or, rather, he had ordered someone to find someone to do it. It was worth nothing to the Emperor in the state it was in now. Rosha had the technical expertise that was sorely needed by the Empire, so he would have to get it back up to speed. He couldn't risk losing this position. He knew the invasion hadn't gone well. It had been a bit heavy-handed.

But all in all, he was doing well. Very well.

A passing cloud rendered the window opaque, and he saw himself reflected. For a moment, he looked old. There had been too many long nights lately. He had shadows under his eyes, and was that a sagging at his jawline? Politics could age you. But politicians couldn't afford to look old. He'd have to find time to sneak away and tighten up a few things. Soon.

Bog swiveled back and forth in the chair, his buoyant mood flattened. Just when he started to think he had his hands full of riches, he would suddenly remember something he didn't have, and he would crash back down into unhappiness again.

It was a lonely feeling.

It was all Astri's fault. He'd had a family, and she'd stolen it.

He'd won the political game, but somehow Astri had outsmarted him and spirited Lune away. He had spies working for him, trying to track her down, but she'd simply vanished from the Fountain Towers in Sath, flying off with a mysterious group, no doubt helped by the resistance.

He reached for his comlink and contacted Sano Sauro. Sauro had messed up badly and had been demoted, but Bog had learned never to kick down the ladder that had boosted him to the top. You never knew when you'd need the ladder again.

Sauro took his communication immediately, which

was pleasant. Now that Bog was Imperial governor, he wouldn't have to scrounge for attention.

Sauro was still a Senator because he could be counted on to vote strictly as the Emperor wanted him to, but he was no longer head of powerful committees, no longer a known politician with Palpatine's ear. Now he was merely in charge of the Imperial Naval Academy, which amused Bog to no end. Sauro was practically a nursemaid!

"Hello, Bog," Sauro said. "How is the governorship coming?"

Bog could hear the poison in his tone. Sauro was probably being eaten alive by jealousy. He'd thought he was smarter than Bog and would rise faster under the new government. What he hadn't valued was Bog's gut instincts. That made him smarter than all the rest of those know-it-alls.

"Coming along," Bog answered shortly. "Lots to do, busy time here. Trying to unite the planet, get them on board with the Empire."

"Of course."

"Any word on our project?"

"None. But I've tapped into the SAM database."

"What's that?"

"Suspicious Movement. Acronym SM. Nickname SAM. Stormtroopers and spies patrol Coruscant and keep their eyes open for suspicious activity. Do spot ID checks. It also goes on within worlds occupied by the

Empire. Governors set up the programs. They all go into one database and are cross-referenced and cross-checked. Then the head security officer decides on surveillance. I have clearance for the database now. I thought you'd know about SAM, Bog."

Sauro was leaning on his name, just a little bit. Just to show that they were still close associates. Bog wondered if he could ask Sauro to call him Governor.

"Oh, of course," he said quickly. "I just didn't get the lingo."

"Right. Anyway, I've got reports coming in daily, and I go through them personally. Any leads, I'll let you know."

"How'd you do that? Get access to the database? Let's face it, your clearance must have been bumped down to almost zero, Sano-Mano." Bog allowed himself a small laugh.

"This is a naval academy," Sauro said in a voice like a carbon-freezer. "I'm still heading the search for any Force-adepts to join it. I have a valuable friendship with Hydra."

The new Grand Inquisitor. How had Sauro managed it? He wasn't a guy you'd want to spend time with. Yet he managed to collect more favors and alliances than even Bog. Which was one reason to keep him happy.

"All right, then. Keep me in the know. And I'll pass on what a good job you're doing, next time I speak to Emperor Palpatine." Bog didn't usually speak to him, actually. But he was sure he would be, now that he was governor of an important system.

"Your generosity has always been overwhelming," Sauro said.

Bog felt flattered, even if he wasn't sure Sauro was being sincere. "Well, you know, the galaxy is big. Lots going on. We've got to keep each other in the loop. Help where we can."

"I'll be in touch."

Bog sensed that Sauro was about to sign off, so he quickly turned off his comlink so he could be the one to break the communication. Then he stabbed at the button for his assistant and asked him to find out why that SAM program hadn't been set up on Rosha. Unless it already had been, and the notation was buried in those reports he kept meaning to read.

Until then, he had Sauro on the line.

CHAPTER TWELVE

"I haven't been lucky since the Emperor took over," Solace said in a low tone to her companions. "I forgot what it feels like."

"It feels gleaming good," Clive said. "That's all I know. It's about time we caught a break."

He and Astri huddled with Solace in an alley. Clive had investigated some old contacts on Coruscant. One of the contacts had clued him in on a network of residence inns that would accept those on the run from the Empire. The group had left surveillance devices outside of each inn. Three levels below the Orange District, they hit paydirt.

It was nothing more than a shadow on the surveillance playback. A figure who leaped from a building a hundred meters away, landed lightly on the roof, then entered the building through an open window. Solace had seen the image and breathed *Jedi*. Immediately they had staked it out. No one had come in or out, through the front door or the windows or the roof.

"It's time to take a look," Solace said. "I doubt I can surprise a Jedi, but if I can get close enough they'll see that I'm a Jedi, too. I'd like to avoid tangling with one unnecessarily."

"Good point," Clive said. "You go first."

Solace arched an eyebrow at him, then Force-leaped to a ledge fifty meters up.

"Show-off," Clive said.

From high above, Solace looked down on Astri and Clive. She hoped they would stay out of the way.

From that vantage point, she spied the window she'd seen on the surveillance feed. Solace leaped over the distance and into the open window.

She stood in a narrow hallway, listening to the quality of the silence. It was a trick she'd honed on countless, tedious sessions at the Temple. She'd only been a human. She didn't have the kind of extrasensory powers she'd seen in other species. So she'd worked on her senses for endless hours. She'd discovered that her hearing was above average, so she'd focused on that. She'd drilled and drilled, entering thousands of different sounds into the computer, turning down the volume lower and lower to identify them, until she could hear a fly land on a wall twenty meters away.

Concentrate. Differentiate. The slight hum of the air

control vents, the distant whine of the lift tube. A cough behind the door of 1257. Someone turned over on a sleep couch in the room directly opposite her. In the room next to that, a towel slipped off a rod and fell to the floor. It was picked up and re-hung.

Then she heard what she was waiting for.

The slither of rough fabric against the leather of a belt as someone moved. The slight, unmistakable metallic click as an object was unclipped.

He knew she was here.

Solace went carefully down the hallway, stopping outside the door she wanted. There was only one way to announce herself, one way to let the being on the other side of the door know she meant him no harm.

She unclipped her lightsaber, activated it, and buried it in the door.

A heartbeat later, three things happened simultaneously. A lightsaber came through the door from the other side.

Well, hello, she said in her head.

She was still smiling as stormtroopers charged out of the lift tube. At the same moment, Clive and Astri climbed in the hallway window.

"Stormtroopers!" Astri shouted.

"No kidding!" Solace yelled back.

The blasterfire streaked down the hallway. Solace pulled her lightsaber out of the molten metal doorway and began advancing, her lightsaber dancing. She didn't know what the Jedi on the other side of the door would do, but a little help would be nice.

But no one arrived.

The stormtroopers released two droidekas in wheel mode. No Jedi wanted to tangle with a droideka. They were hard to shut down, and their double-barreled blaster cannonfire could give even a Jedi a battle headache. Solace leaped out of the way, trying to figure out a way to get past the deflector shields without being blown to bits.

Another stormtrooper rolled a grenade down toward her. Solace kicked it back with one foot while leaping up to take down the seeker droid overhead. More stormtroopers poured out of the lift tube. The grenade exploded, sending three of them flying.

She certainly had her hands full.

Thanks a lot, whoever you are, Solace thought. The Jedi had obviously escaped out of the room through the window.

Well, the galaxy had changed, and the remaining Jedi had changed along with it. It was every Jedi for himself or herself now.

Wasn't that what she'd told Ferus?

A spasm of blasterfire came a little close for comfort. Her battle mind had slipped for a moment. It wasn't like her to start *thinking* in the middle of a battle. That could be deadly.

Suddenly a tall human male came swinging out of the turbolift shaft. Solace didn't get a glimpse of his face, hidden in the shadows of a hood. But his lightsaber work was extraordinary. The stormtroopers were surrounded now, and Solace and the mysterious Jedi moved as a team. The tall Jedi was obviously familiar with droidekas. He charged, his lightsaber in a spinning arc, and with deft precision struck them at a vulnerable point Solace hadn't known existed, underneath their shell, near their repulsorlift motors.

The Jedi leaped over the remaining stormtroopers and landed by her side. She had a quick impression of chromium eyes, pale skin, and a melancholy face.

He jerked his chin toward the window in the hallway, where Clive and Astri had taken shelter in a doorway.

She read his intent without words. It was time to get out of there.

They raced down the hallway together, still deflecting fire from the remaining stormtroopers. Solace signaled to Clive and Astri, who leaped out the window, using their liquid cables. Solace and the Jedi followed. They landed on the roof next door and raced across it, dodging vents and debris.

The Jedi took the lead. It was obvious that he had planned an escape route. He led them to an empty lift tube shaft that had a small door on the roof. Using their liquid cables, Astri and Clive rappelled down the shaft. Solace and the Jedi jumped.

The tall Jedi led them into a service level of the building, where laundry and storage were held. They ran down a twisting maze of hallways that were like tunnels. He pried off a grid in the wall and hurried them inside. Crawling, they followed the pipe until he pointed above. Solace pushed the grid out. They climbed out into an unfamiliar alley.

Stained with rust and mud, the four regarded one another. The Jedi said nothing. Solace didn't recognize him. She saw now that his hair was white and cut close to his skull. Despite his large frame, he held himself gracefully.

"Aren't you going to introduce yourself?" Solace asked.

"Ry-Gaul," he said. His voice was low and softer than she'd expected.

"My name as a Jedi was Fy-Tor Ana," Solace said. "Now I am Solace."

"Are there others?" Ry-Gaul asked. "I have been alone."

"Not many," Solace said. "I was contacted by Ferus Olin. He's trying to gather any Jedi who are left. He was —"

"— Siri Tachi's apprentice." Ry-Gaul's face underwent a change. The severe lines smoothed out. It was close to a smile, but not quite. "Ferus," he said. "I was on several missions with him. With my Padawan, Tru Veld."

Solace nodded. She had never kept track of the Padawans. She had chosen not to take an apprentice. But Ferus had mentioned Tru Veld. He'd been a friend. Ferus had found his lightsaber at the Temple.

"Do you know something about him?" Ry-Gaul asked, his tone suddenly urgent.

"I know he is dead," she said. "I'm sorry." It wasn't like her to tell someone she was sorry about something she had nothing to do with. But something about this large man of few words made her be a little more polite than she usually was.

Ry-Gaul bowed his head. "It is what I expected. Yet it is hard to hear it."

Solace bent her head close to him. "Out of all the beings in the universe, I think I am one of the few who can say I know how you feel."

CHAPTER THIRTEEN

Ferus didn't know if it would work. But he eliminated doubt from his mind. If he wondered if it would work, it wouldn't.

He turned to the stormtroopers. "You can leave me here. I can find my way alone."

The stormtrooper turned to the others. "We can leave him here. He can find his way alone."

Was it really that simple?

Simple, it is. Belief, it is.

To reach the point where it was simple — *that* was hard.

Ferus didn't push his luck. He walked quickly away, down the path, then doubled back to cross the garrison from the rear, where its perimeter was closest to the street. He quickly crossed to a busy boulevard. He expected to be stopped at any moment. Instead he was able to lose himself in the crowd.

He wasn't followed; he was sure of that. He walked down the familiar streets. Despite the fact that he was worried and frazzled and worn out, he felt something in him lift. Just to be walking these streets, without an escort. Just to be himself, no matter how short a time.

Before they had both left for the Clone Wars, he and Roan had talked about what they would do if they were separated, if Bellassa were overrun, if . . . *There were so many ifs in those days*, Ferus thought. But not nearly as many as now. So they had staked out several areas in and around Ussa for a meeting, then assigned each place a code. They also chose several places in the city and several methods to alert each other. Ferus hadn't forgotten any of it.

Roan had indicated to him to proceed to their third secret meeting place, in the Cloud Lake District, near their old office. It was a large, bustling café. Ferus entered, carefully keeping his hood over his face so that he wouldn't be recognized. He knew this café well. Roan had no doubt chosen it because it was always crowded, and it had three entrances and exits.

Roan was waiting.

Ferus kept moving, but his eyes blurred and it was hard to see. The café was full, and it was a swirl of color and motion, of sound that hit his ears in a continuous roar. He felt overwhelmed by the sensation. It was home, and there was Roan, waiting. For one impossible moment it was as though nothing had changed.

It was not the way a Jedi was supposed to see or hear. It was not the way a Jedi was supposed to feel.

A Jedi shouldn't want to go back.

A Jedi should accept where he was.

He was conscious of Dona at a nearby table. That helped to steady him. He was able to survey the room, look for exits and strategies should they be discovered. Only then did he look back and feel pleasure at seeing Roan again.

He sat at the table. "It was so strange to see you sitting here."

Roan knew exactly what he meant. "Like nothing had changed."

"When everything has."

Roan's sad eyes were the same clear green-gray. He was growing healthier by the day. The torture procedures he'd undergone at the Imperial prison had not changed him as Ferus had feared they would.

"Trever?" Ferus asked.

"Is fine. He's here, on Bellassa."

Ferus nodded. The relief he felt made his legs feel weak.

"He came to the base in a new ship, thinking we'd all welcome him with open arms. Well, we welcomed him."

Ferus smiled. "At least he came back."

"That's what *he* said."

Roan allowed a moment to pass, a moment of shared silence. His hands rested on the table, one hand cupped inside the other in a way that only Roan had.

"Why did you call for me?" Ferus asked. He didn't know how much time they had, but it wasn't much.

"The Eleven are concerned with your role on Bellassa," Roan said. "Sentiment in Ussa is running against you. I realize that for you that's a secondary consideration. But it is a blow to the resistance movement. And we've had many of those lately. Are you learning anything we can use?"

"Not yet," Ferus admitted. "I'm kept on a very short leash. But I did get a quick peek at Vader's code cylinder files. There's something on it called Twilight that I want to look into. A large-scale operation. And then there's the question of the factory retooling here in Ussa. What's really going on with that?"

"Are the two related?"

"Could be, but I don't think so. Twilight has all the earmarks of a snare operation, like Order 66. The plans here involve something big, some kind of technology that the Empire is developing that's so secret only a few at the top know about it."

"Who? Vader?"

"Vader, for one. Moff Tarkin, too."

"Tarkin. He's a nasty piece of work. Seems to have his fingers in plenty of pies." Roan thought for a moment. "Can you get us in to where they keep records?"

"I don't know. I'll have to do some investigating first."

"They'd have to keep some sort of files at the factory itself. At the beginning of an operation, things can be messy — systems aren't in place, the chain of command isn't quite set. We'd have to get in, probably at night, and snoop around."

Ferus nodded. "If we find out what it is, I'm ready to quit. I'm done."

"Tired of Vader's company already?"

He grimaced. "If we can expose what they're doing here, suspicion will fall on me. They won't trust me with anything after that. And if I can walk away and go underground here in Bellassa . . ."

"It will embarrass them." Roan nodded. "I think you've put in enough time."

"It's just that . . . Twilight. Whatever that is. I need to find out."

"There are other ways. You don't have to be in Vader's pocket. They might never give you the clearance to find anything significant anyway."

"That's what I thought. But . . . if I stop working for the Empire, I can't stay on Bellassa. I'll need to go back to the base for a time. Then head out and look for more Jedi."

"I know," Roan said. "I'm glad you brought that up. I've finally seen your secret base, and can I tell you this? You need help."

Ferus let the implications sink in. He knew what it meant. Roan was offering to come with him.

"You always said your job was here, on Bellassa."

"My job is to help you," Roan said. "If that means helping with your crackpot plan to find the Jedi, I'll do it. We're part of the same struggle now. I'm replaceable here on Bellassa. There are those who can take my place. You need help there. I agree with this Flame person when it comes to one thing: We have to look at galactic resistance. It's the only way. We can't do it only on one planet. Sooner or later, what you're doing will link up with what's being done elsewhere."

"I hope so," Ferus said. "I'm just glad you're coming."

"I'm coming. But first let's do what we can here. Contact me when you come up with a way to get in. I'll assemble a team."

They stood. They couldn't risk staying any longer. Ferus again felt the loneliness wrap around his heart. There were so many things he wanted to talk to Roan about, and couldn't. Not just about logistics, but feelings. One thing about war — there was never enough time.

A quick grasp of each other's upper arms in their old greeting, a look into each other's eyes, and Ferus turned on his heel and was gone.

CHAPTER FOURTEEN

Keets collapsed on a bench, breathing hard. "I didn't . . . sign on . . . to the resistance . . . to be"—He leaned his head back and let out an explosive puff of air — "a nanny!"

"He's a handful," Curran said, with a fond look at Lune.

They sat in a small park on the uppermost level of Coruscant, near the Senate District. Lune had begged to be allowed to play, and the Orange District was hardly suitable. Astri had given reluctant permission. She'd wanted Lune to get some sun, despite her worries. He'd been on an asteroid for weeks without light.

Keets and Curran had decided on a neighborhood popular with families so they could lose themselves in the crowds. "Can't we get a droid for this job?" Keets wondered. "Some Class Three Nanny with a nice disposition?"

"Dex asked us to do it," Curran said. "Besides, a droid won't keep an eye out for stormtroopers."

"That kid could probably program it, too," Keets said. "That kid could probably do anything he set his mind to."

They watched as Lune joined in a game some boys and girls had improvised on one of the playground installations, a large plastoid power slide that sent off puffs of air to speed descent. The group had lined up on the various chutes and were racing to see who could get down fastest. The laughter traveled over to Keets and Curran.

"C'mon," Curran said. "This has got to make even you smile."

"I don't go gooey over kids," Keets said. "I may no longer be a galactically famous journalist, I may have to scrounge and shrink from every glowlamp, and I may be living with a former pusher of bantha stew, but I haven't sunk that low."

"You're a very cynical human," Curran said serenely.

Keets put an arm over the bench and looked over at a towering statue of Emperor Palpatine. "Galactic City used to be a fairly nice place."

"You mean *Imperial* City," Curran corrected.

"I'll never call it that," Keets replied. "Emperor Palpa-creep can rename it, but I don't have to listen to him. Hey, what's that kid up to now?" Keets asked, looking over at Lune.

The boy had opened the control panel of the power slide and was making an adjustment.

"Should we . . ." Keets said.

Curran shook his head, grinning. "I say we just watch."

Lune scrambled back up the ramp to the very top of the slide. He positioned himself in front of the jets. The sensor picked up his presence, and a blast of air sent him straight up into the air. Instead of landing, Lune hung there.

Keets's jaw dropped. Curran half rose.

Lune did a somersault in the air. He looked down at the other kids with their upturned faces and stuck out his tongue.

"Curran . . ." Keets said warningly.

"He's okay," Curran said. He had relaxed back into his seat.

"That's not what I mean." Keets nudged him and pointed.

A squad of stormtroopers on patrol was crossing the street.

"What should we do?" Curran asked. His furry face, normally the color of a roasted nut, paled.

"If we run toward him, we'll just attract their attention," Keets said. "They won't notice. Nobody notices kids."

Lune landed on the bottom of the slide, then leaped up again.

The other kids screamed at him with glee, clapping their hands.

The head stormtrooper looked up.

"Uh-oh," Keets breathed.

Lune jumped down on the slide, caught another blast of air, and used it and the Force to leap even higher. He landed on top of a neighboring terrace, then used the momentum to leap back again and land in front of the cheering children.

Keets could see only the helmets of the stormtroopers move as they tracked Lune.

"Let's get him," Keets said.

They walked over to Lune. Keets spoke softly. "Time to go, kiddo."

"No!" the other kids all shouted. "Show us how you did that!"

"Sorry!" Curran tried to extricate himself from the crowd of kids.

The squad of stormtroopers started to head over.

Keets dug into his pocket and extricated the bag of sweets he'd bought from a vendor. He threw them into the air. "Have fun!"

The kids scattered, chasing the candy. Keets urged Lune forward. Curran flanked him, and they quickly hustled him out of the playground. They turned down the first street they came to, then the next, and the next, until they were lost in the crowd and they knew they hadn't been followed.

They looked at each other over Lune's head.

It hardly mattered that they'd escaped.

Lune had been noticed.

CHAPTER FIFTEEN

Ferus slipped back into the garrison and went to the quarters that had been assigned to him. He sat on the chair, thinking.

Conduits and modular components for artificial atmospheres on an unprecedented scale.

Ferus knew that *artificial atmospheres* could mean anything. It could be a small city or a large ship or a building. Was the Empire building a massive prison? New headquarters?

Not headquarters, Ferus thought. The Emperor had retooled the Senate to his liking. He had no need of new headquarters. And besides, such a project wouldn't have to be secret.

. . . an unprecedented scale . . .

Ferus didn't like the sound of that.

For the next three days, Ferus was escorted to the factory along with the scientists. Bellassan factories had always combined their research laboratories with their manufacturing facilities in the same compound, so the scientists already had some resources to begin. Ferus found himself with the menial tasks of checking off the delivery of various supplies to the labs, like dataports and durasheets. Since nothing classified had begun, reporters from the HoloNet were given free rein.

Ferus was along as a "facilitator," meaning that he attended meetings where nothing much was decided in order to be in more news reports about the amazing Empire and what it could accomplish on Bellassa. Nowhere was it mentioned what the scientists would be working on, except in the vaguest terms.

At least in his position he was able to watch. He noted that Moff Tarkin often went into one particular office, where senior officers sat in front of computer consoles. He guessed they were setting up programs and organizational structures. A nervous-looking team of Bellassan architects were brought in, no doubt to "facilitate" the conversion.

Ferus tried to find a way to be alone with the scientists, but they were closely guarded. He could sense the misery of some of them, but he could tell that several others had volunteered for this mission. One scientist from Eriadu seemed especially eager to impress Tarkin. The sad-faced woman in the burgundy tunic kept to herself, but her misery was like a cloud around her.

Ferus's only hope was to get into that room.

On the third afternoon, he was beginning to despair when, on his way to leave with a troop of officers, he saw the factory caretaker passing on a repulsorlift cart. Ferus made a small sign of acknowledgment, but the caretaker turned his head.

Puzzled at his reaction, Ferus walked out with the officers to the main docking bay. It was empty.

"The ship was supposed to be here waiting," the senior officer said, annoyed. He took out his comlink. "What's the status on the transport back to the garrison?" he barked.

"There was a shutdown on all air traffic while they made the trial run of supply ships for the Despayre run," a voice said.

"Get a ship here now!" the officer ordered testily.

Despayre. Ferus had heard that name before, when he'd been at the Imperial prison planet in the Outer Rim. The prisoners had worked in a huge factory. They never knew what they were working on, but he'd discovered that the parts were being shipped to a facility on Despayre.

It was too much of a coincidence. Was it a piece of the puzzle?

Ferus's gaze wandered over to the translucent doors at one end of the platform. They opened into the deserted garden.

"I'll wait in there," he told the officer, who grimaced but nodded.

Ferus waved his hand over the sensor and walked into the garden. In a moment, another door opened, and, just as he'd hoped, the caretaker entered. He didn't glance at Ferus but immediately put down his tools and knelt down to weed around a grouping of tender plants.

"I'm glad they let you keep the garden," Ferus said, coming up behind him.

The caretaker didn't look up. "They? Seems to me you're one of them now."

Ferus couldn't miss the contempt in the man's tone.

"I didn't recognize you at first," the caretaker continued, his hands in the soil as he carefully pulled out a weed. "Now I know who you are. You fought them and defied them and made them look like fools. And now you're one of them."

Ferus took a breath, considering. He was getting nowhere here. He had to find a way. He had to trust someone.

The caretaker stood, dusting off his trousers. "We were a unique world. We resisted to every last man, woman, and child. They couldn't find their spies here, their betrayers. We protected you and all of the Eleven, even as they grew to number hundreds. Every family had someone working for the resistance. Maybe . . ." — The caretaker looked steadily at his flowers, never at Ferus, and shook his head — ". . . maybe you were only the first to fall. But that doesn't mean I have to be civil to you."

"I don't expect politeness," Ferus said. "Just honesty. And maybe . . . help."

"I have no help to give you."

Ferus bent down and carefully placed his hand near a small lizard that was sitting on a leaf. It crawled onto his palm. Bright green, it blinked at the two of them. Ferus brought the lizard over to a bright orange blossom and placed it there. The lizard's skin began to blush. Its pigment changed until it blazed in the same bright color as the blossom. The transformation was so complete that it was impossible to pick out the lizard now. He'd disappeared against the flower.

Ferus looked steadily at the caretaker. "It looks like a blossom," he said. "But the lizard is still a lizard."

He saw that the caretaker knew what he was trying to tell him without words. The lizard could change his skin, could blend in, in order to survive. So could Ferus. But that didn't make him part of the Empire.

"Don't you wish," Ferus said, "you knew what they were doing here?"

The caretaker didn't say anything for a long moment. Then he bent down to pull up a weed. "I know there are droids who do this work," he said. "But I don't trust them to do the job right. Droids can malfunction."

Ferus nodded. "Happens all the time."

"Even security droids. They can go off-line for no reason, for fifteen minutes at a time. Takes me that long to reset the system." He tossed a weed into his basket. "They have me in charge of security here, mostly because there's nothing to steal, so far. I'm at the east end of the factory. It's quiet down there. I just monitor the security system. Round about three in the morning, I get too tired to even make my rounds."

He picked up his tools. "Got to take work where you can get it, these days. I just keep my head down and don't make a fuss. About anything."

"Good policy." Ferus glanced over at the loading dock as a transport began to land. "Well, I'd better get going."

"My name's Russell," the caretaker said. He looked at him for the first time. "I'm glad to meet you, Ferus Olin."

Flame was meeting with Wil, Amie, Trever, Dona, and several members of the Eleven when Roan and Dona returned to the safe house.

"This is remarkable," Amie told him when he came in. "Flame has enormous resources at her disposal. Her ideas about networking planetary resistance are quite detailed."

"I can go over what you missed, if you'd like," Flame told Roan.

"I'm sorry, I don't have time. I need to ask you to leave for a few minutes."

Roan's authority was absolute, and no one questioned him. Flame stood and walked toward the door, but hesitated. "I can help," she said. "Whatever it is, I can help."

"This is Bellassan business," Roan said.

"But my point is that it's not just Bellassan business," Flame said. She linked her hands together and held them up. "Every planet's resistance should be part of the next one, and so on."

"She's right, Roan," Amie said.

"I appreciate your philosophy," Roan said. "It's a subject for discussion. But right now I need a closed meeting."

Flame nodded her head and slipped out the door.

"Why'd you have to do that, Roan?" Trever burst out. "She could help!"

Roan gave him a look that silenced him. "This is too important to risk, Trever. Ferus has contacted me."

"Maybe Ferus shouldn't be the one that you're trusting," Trever said heatedly.

"He *had* to send you away, Trever," Roan said.

"That isn't what this is about."

"He thought he was protecting you. You were the first thing he asked about when he saw me." Roan's voice was gentle. "If trust were easy, it wouldn't be so valuable. Think of the man you know, and ask yourself if he could betray us."

Trever couldn't hold Roan's gaze. He ducked his head. He felt ashamed. There was so much trust in this room that he was able to connect with it again.

Wil and Amie looked at Roan. "What happened?" Wil asked him.

"Ferus contacted me. It's tonight," he said. "He has some sort of contact at the factory who will help us."

"Good," Wil said.

"The question is, who should go? We only have a fifteen-minute window. Ferus's contact will shut down security at three in the morning. We could open this up to more members of the Eleven, but it would take time to set up. I think a three-person team makes sense. We can do more exploring that way. We'll hit the computer system and search the main office. Wil, you're out because of your injury. And, Dona, there's nobody better I'd want watching my back, but you don't have experience with this kind of thing. So anybody want to volunteer?"

Everyone raised a hand. Even Dona.

Roan smiled and leaned back. "All I can say is, it's good to be back on Bellassa."

"I should go," Trever said. "I know how to work with Ferus. I know what he's thinking, and believe it or not, I can obey orders."

"I want to go," Amie said. "I have got the most scientific background. If we're lucky enough to get into the computer files, I can translate any technical jargon."

Amie and Roan looked at Trever.

"Don't say I'm too young, because that always sends me into a full-scale laser cannon mode," Trever said. "Besides, I'm better at sneaking in and out of places than all of you put together."

"Can't argue with that," Roan said.

"All right, it's decided," Wil said. "Roan, Amie, and Trever. Tonight."

CHAPTER SIXTEEN

In his rough traveler's clothes, Ry-Gaul looked like countless others, beings uprooted by the Clone Wars and the Imperial takeover and looking for a place to call home again. But as she walked beside him, Solace could feel the strength of the Force.

"How did you escape Order Sixty-six?" Solace asked.

"I was on a secret mission," he said. "Only Yoda knew about it. I was on a world in the Outer Rim, under cover. I left Tru Veld at the Temple. He was working on a valuable research project."

"The Temple was invaded," Solace said. "Everyone was killed."

Ry-Gaul closed his eyes for a moment. "I thought he'd be safer at the Temple. If he'd come with me, he would be alive."

"Decisions are not for regret, but for understanding," Solace said. The familiar words of a Jedi saying felt soothing in her mouth.

"I heard the lies the Empire was spreading about the Jedi one day in a cantina," he said. "I realized that everyone I knew was dead." He looked down at his large, white hands. "I wanted to go back to Coruscant immediately, but I was almost caught at a checkpoint as I tried to make my way there. A couple — a man and wife — rescued me. They smuggled me back to their homeworld and offered me a place to stay. They were scientists. They found me a new identity, and I was readying myself to leave again when they disappeared. I've been looking for them ever since."

"Well, you've attracted the notice of the Empire," Solace told him.

"I know. But I couldn't stop looking. The more I looked, the more I uncovered. Other scientists are missing. Some go willingly. Others seem to have been forced. And I'm sure the Empire is behind it."

"They're using them for something," Solace said, looking at the others. "We have to tell Dex about this."

"Ferus should know about it, too," Clive said. "It might help him on Bellassa."

"We're close to the Orange District," Solace said. "You'll be safe there."

They took a lift tube down a hundred levels to the Orange District. They walked quickly through the passages, taking the smaller streets. They approached the long, serpentine alley where Dex's safe house was located.

"Look, there's Lune," Astri said, a surge of happiness lighting her voice.

She started toward the group. Solace tensed. She noticed that Curran and Keets were careful to keep him in front of them, shielding him from the street. Instead of turning into the alley, they went left.

"Astri, wait," Solace said. "Something's wrong."

It was an absolute rule that anyone who suspected they were followed must not turn down the alley. It could expose Dex's safe house.

Worried now, Solace split off from the group and quickened her pace.

She was too late.

The stormtroopers burst out of an unmarked airspeeder and released seeker droids with blasters into the air. The blasterfire caught Curran, who went down. Keets wheeled around, holding Lune tightly against him. Solace leaped toward the airspeeder, her lightsaber held aloft.

Behind her she could sense Ry-Gaul moving. She knew he was positioning himself to flank her.

But they were too far away, and too late. Keets was overpowered by the stormtroopers. Lune was wrenched away. The boy didn't make a sound.

It was Astri, on her knees, whose wailing cry of anguish split the air as Lune disappeared into the crowded sky.

CHAPTER SEVENTEEN

Ferus waited by the garden wall. It didn't take long until three shapes materialized out of the darkness. Roan, Trever, and Amie.

"You took your time finding me again," he told Trever. He squeezed the boy's shoulders, glad to see him looking so well.

"You're the one who keeps disappearing." Trever felt better, just seeing Ferus once more. He couldn't believe he had suspected him. One suspicion had led to another until his mind was crammed full of doubt. He didn't know how it had started, but he was glad it was over.

"This door," Ferus said, leading the way.

As soon as they were inside, Ferus took them to the central office where he'd seen Moff Tarkin. Then he pointed out the scientist's meeting rooms and labs.

"I'll take the labs," Amie said.

"I'm going to check out the computer in the hangar," Trever said. "Flight records might tell us something."

"I'll try the main computer," Roan said. "Come on, Ferus."

It was like old times. Ferus and Roan hit the keyboards under pressure, trying to track down secrets. Once it had been from dishonest multisystem corporations, and now it was from an empire they were certain was choking the life and heart of the galaxy.

"I'm going to key in *Despayre* and see what I get," Roan said. "After you mentioned it, I researched it but didn't find much. Outer Rim planet, in the Horuz system, a penal colony . . . a curious lack of real information."

"I'm going to take a look at Tarkin's files, see if I can access anything," Ferus said.

For long seconds there was only the clicking of keys and buttons.

Suddenly, Roan whistled. Ferus knew that whistle. Roan was busy whipping out his datapad.

"That probably has a safety wipe on it," Ferus warned. "If you try to download information, it will erase itself."

"Disabled it. Don't you remember how very good I am at this?" Roan grinned as he flipped through the data. "This is interesting. . . . I've got a memo from Tarkin to the factory manager telling him to bypass normal safeguards for any workers. We can release this information and bust a big smoking hole in their 'we're here for the betterment of Bellassa' spacejunk."

Ferus returned his attention to his own search. "Weapons delivery system," he said. "That's what they must be working on. I've got orders for high-functioning engineering droids. . . . Whoa — a shipment of Loquasin and Titroxinate." He paused. "Some of these memos have been forwarded to ZA."

"Friend of yours?"

"There's only one ZA. Jenna Zan Arbor. Galactic criminal and all-around vicious rival."

"Sounds like they're working on weapons here as well as infrastructure. That's totally against what they said."

"With false labels . . . it's all undercover."

Just then Amie entered. "We've got about four more minutes," she said. "I'm finding out some strange stuff. It's not so much what they're working on as the scale of it. Like they're planning to take over an entire planet and redo its infrastructure or something . . ."

"Take a look at this," Ferus said, tilting the data-screen toward her.

She read it swiftly. "This is similar to some of the methods they've used on torture victims, Roan included," she said. "Totally against the regulations the Senate passed generations ago."

"The Emperor doesn't believe in following regula-tions," Roan said. "He lets the Senate pass them and then ignores them. It's a convenient version of democracy."

"And it's all for the good of the galaxy, remember?" Ferus said. "We'd better get out of here. Time's up. I think we have enough. Where's Trever?"

"Late, as usual," Roan said, shutting down the computer. "Let's meet him at the door."

Running now, with the sense of the chrono ticking the time away, they reached the exit door, but no one was there.

Roan let out an exasperated sound. They had less than a minute now. Where was Trever?

CHAPTER EIGHTEEN

Trever didn't learn anything on the hangar computer. He wasn't a whiz like Roan. He'd picked up a couple of hacking techniques from Ferus, but he wasn't a mastermind.

So he did what came naturally — he snooped. In his experience, information was often not hidden in computers. It was around the next turning in the hall, or behind a closed door.

He had only ten minutes, but he could cover a lot of ground in ten minutes. Trever hoofed it down the hallway, peeking into offices and laboratories, looking for something. He didn't know what it was, but he'd know when he found it.

He turned a corner and stopped. He was at the opposite end of the factory complex now. It should be deserted. But his senses told him otherwise. It wasn't as though he heard something or saw something. He *felt* something.

He shook his head. Was that Force bunkum starting to work on him? No, it wasn't that. It was his street instincts. He trusted them just as much as Ferus-Wan trusted his Force.

He stopped and held his breath. Closed his eyes.

Whoosh, ah. Whoosh, ah.

Well, this was a new moon day. Darth Vader. Just what he needed.

He shrank back, moving quietly. There was an equipment closet to his right, and if he could just sneak into it and get out his comlink to warn the others, he just might make it out of here alive. Except that they were on comlink silence, because they figured communications could be intercepted in an Imperial facility.

He eased into the closet and kept the door open a crack. How lucky could a guy get, meeting up with Lord-on-High Vader again?

He watched as Vader swept down the hall, waved his gloved hand over a sensor, and walked into an office.

Russell Wake had always tried to stay out of politics. He was fortunate to live on Bellassa, for it made it easy, at least before the Clone Wars. Rulers were elected, and the normal ebb and flow of scandal and missed opportunities, corruption, and grandstanding, was easy to ignore. Even when the Clone Wars began, he found himself able to avoid taking a position. He couldn't get excited about fighting Separatists, for they were fighting a Senate that was riddled with greed and corruption. Who could say they were wrong?

Then the Empire took over. And suddenly everything he valued in his life was thrown away. The Emperor turned his stone-gray gaze on Bellassa and deemed it worthy of conquest and example. He wanted to install a governor, and the Bellassans objected. And once that objection registered as solid opposition, the Empire had to come down on them.

They had underestimated the opposition.

And though he tried to keep out of it, Russell Wake's old heart was stirred. Freedom became more than a concept to him; it was a reality as firm as the turborake he held in his hands.

The things he counted on had disappeared. The quarrelsome politicians, silenced. The press, shut down. Once the Empire had moved its garrison in and controlled the government, people were imprisoned without trial or charges; fear ruled the city, and those who ran the government were replaced if they protested.

But if Russell was moved to care about all this, it didn't mean he ever wanted to fight it. Resistance members had physical courage. Russell could show no mercy when it came to a weed choking his silverbloom bush, but he knew very well he would crumble under any real danger. The idea of joining a resistance movement was never in his plans.

Until he walked through a door and saw Ferus Olin.

So now he sat here, his palms slick with sweat, and waited for Ferus and his crew to do whatever they needed. He had given them fifteen minutes. Surely he could hold his nerves steady for fifteen minutes.

If only they weren't such long minutes. . . .

His door hissed open, and he shot out of his chair so fast he smashed his knees on the console.

His worst fear stood in his doorway.

"You seem . . . nervous this evening," Darth Vader said.

His heart was pounding, slamming against his chest so hard, surely it was visible. He couldn't seem to find his breath. "It's a long night," he said.

Somehow, even while his heart was slamming and his breath was gone and his mouth was as dry as a desert planet, somehow he managed to stand up, right in front of the console where the indicator light shone yellow, indicating a problem with security, and block it.

"You were seen talking to Ferus Olin today," Darth Vader said.

He pretended to look blank for a moment. "Oh, yes." So this was what it was, just a regular inquisition. He'd heard Vader liked to question beings at odd hours, keep them off balance. He cleared his throat. *Don't clear your throat, it makes you sound guilty.* "In the garden. For a few minutes."

"What did you discuss?"

"Gardening."

Suddenly Russell felt an odd constriction in his throat. His hand flew up to loosen his tunic.

"It is not your clothing," Darth Vader said.

The constriction grew. He was croaking out a breath now.

It wasn't as though Russell's life flashed before his eyes. It wasn't as though he remembered everything from birth until this moment. He thought of his wife, and he thought of his daughter, and he thought of the courage he thought he didn't have, and suddenly, there it was, in his hands. Courage and defiance and pride.

"I have nothing . . . to tell. . . ."

He stared into the black visor, heard the rushing sound of Vader's breath. He felt an emptiness, as if the creature so casually choking the life out of him had no feelings about it whatsoever. He closed his eyes so he could block out that merciless void. Instead he pictured the things that nourished him. His garden. His wife. His daughter.

He was traveling down a rushing tunnel of black. Sparks shooting out of his fingers, his heels. No pain now.

He just wished . . . he just wished someone could know this.

He'd found his courage in the end.

* * *

Ferus saw immediately that the hangar was empty. He took off down the hall. He was almost to the northeast section when he saw Trever running full tilt toward him, his hair dripping with sweat.

"Vader," he gasped out.

"Where?"

Trever pointed with his chin. "He went to an office, asked questions about you . . . from some old guy —"

"Russell." Ferus started to take off, but Trever called to him.

"It's too late." Ferus turned. Trever's face was ashen. "He questioned him, but Russell didn't say anything . . . so . . ." Trever gulped in air. "I saw it. I saw it all, Ferus!"

Ferus saw that the boy was close to the edge. He had seen so many things, but he hadn't yet seen this — the casual destruction of a living being, face-to-face, for no other motive than to extract a piece of information.

Ferus grabbed Trever and hurried him toward the laboratory. He brought him to a small room filled with equipment. "Stay here. Don't move. I'll get you when it's safe. And take this." Ferus handed Trever the information chip from Roan's datapad. "Hide it."

"But what . . ."

"Wil has to see it. If I don't come back, get yourself

to the hangar just before daybreak. There will be transports coming in and out. Try to sneak aboard — you're good at that. I should be able to come back and get you."

"But what will you —"

"Trever, there's no time. One of us has to get out. It might have to be you. Just one thing — stay away from Vader!"

Ferus took off. He at least had to ensure Trever's safety. He was too late for Russell.

He ran back the way he had come, thinking fast. He couldn't fight Vader; he didn't have the skill. He would, if it were a last resort. But his best strategy now would be to bluff. He had to remember that as far as Vader knew, he was loyal to the Empire.

He raced down the last hallway, turning toward the door where Roan and Amie waited. He skidded to a halt. Darth Vader stood between him and his friends.

Vader didn't turn. "Ah, Olin has joined us. Perhaps you can explain what these thieves are doing here."

"I was asked by the Emperor to keep an eye on security here," Ferus said, improvising. Vader wouldn't be able to check until later. And later Ferus would be back underground or off-planet.

If it worked.

"I can take them into custody," he said.

Vader half turned. "Do you think I do not recognize

Roan Lands? Do you think I would be foolish enough to let you take him away?"

"He is a former associate, yes, but —"

It happened before he could get out another word. Faster than an eyeblink. Faster than he'd seen anyone move, anyone except Yoda.

The lightsaber hadn't been there, and then it was, and the lightsaber was a blur. Vader moved without seeming to move, and the lightsaber sliced into Roan, straight into his chest. Straight into his heart.

Roan fell to his knees. At first, pain filmed his gaze but he didn't flinch, he just looked at Ferus. Looked long and hard and said many things in the space of a second.

Don't give yourself away for me.

Amie cried out and knelt to support Roan. Ferus ran forward and caught him as he fell. He didn't care about his cover, he didn't even care about Roan's warning, he only knew the remarkable pain he felt.

Roan reached out for Ferus's forearm, his fingers slipping off. Ferus picked up Roan's hand and placed it on his arm. Then he put his hand on Roan's other arm in their private greeting, their private farewell. He squeezed Roan's arm, wishing he could pass his strength into him.

He'd seen enough of death to know it was too late.

"Farewell, brother," he whispered.

He felt Roan's spirit lift, he felt it fly.

And he was left alone.

So alone that there was no thought, only rage so black it blotted everything else out.

He launched himself at Darth Vader, his lightsaber in his hand.

CHAPTER NINETEEN

His lightsaber came down on empty air.

He thought he'd have the element of surprise, at least, but Vader had expected the attack. He had *wanted* it. He had provoked it. He had killed Roan to provoke Ferus. There was no other explanation for it, and it served to fuel Ferus's rage.

Roan had died for *this*?

Ferus heard Amie shout, but he couldn't focus on anything but his own need to plunge his lightsaber deep into Vader. He whirled and attacked again, but Vader again was gone, moving with a speed and lightness that was surprising considering his body armor.

Ferus felt the dark side of the Force fill the air, choking him. And suddenly his body was wrenched forward, and he hung in the air like a puppet. He looked down at Vader's helmet.

"I am bored," Darth Vader said. He placed his glowing lightsaber against Ferus's neck.

Ferus waited to be killed. He looked into that helmet and felt the stirring of something . . . *personal*. A hatred deep in a black heart, a hatred so big it was directed not so much at Ferus but at what he *represented*.

What is the source of his hate?

Stormtroopers suddenly filled the hallway, their blaster rifles held in attack mode. Ferus felt the grip of the Force ease, and he crashed to the floor.

"Take him. And her. And take that one away." Vader's order was crisp.

"And the weapon, sir?"

Vader turned and looked down at the lightsaber hilt still in Ferus's hand. "He can keep it. As a reminder of his failure."

He turned and walked down the hall and disappeared.

The stormtroopers dragged Roan away like a sack of grain.

Ferus felt them lift him, force him to walk alongside Amie. Prison again. Execution, most certainly.

He didn't care.

CHAPTER TWENTY

Trever hadn't strictly told the truth in the meeting with the Eleven. He wasn't that good at obeying orders. He'd never been able to stay put just because someone asked him to. Even Ferus couldn't make him do that.

So he watched from around the corner and saw it all. He saw the shock of Vader's action. He saw Roan crash to his knees. He saw Ferus charge, and he waited for Ferus to die.

He couldn't stop shaking.

He thought he'd seen everything. He thought he could handle anything. But he felt as though his mind had broken after seeing this night.

She found him in the laboratory, a tall, slender woman in a dark-red tunic that reached to her knees. When she opened the door, a shaft of light hit his face. He turned away but didn't move. He couldn't imagine running anymore.

She knelt in front of him. "Well, hello."

He put his face against his knees.

"Security is all over the building," she murmured. "I heard there was a break-in. Some prisoners taken. I'll help you."

He looked up.

"I'm just as much a prisoner as you are," she said. "But I'll try to get you out."

"I'm supposed to go to the hangar," he said. "Before dawn."

"I can do that. I have clearance. Can you walk?"

Of course he could walk. But when he stood, his legs were shaking. Her hand was cool as she curled her fingers around his. She squeezed his hand lightly.

It was that touch that brought him back. He had felt so alone. He had needed to connect to something, even if it was just a touch from a stranger.

She nodded reassuringly at him, and she rolled a cart toward him with a large canister on it. "Can you fit?"

He climbed in. He drew up his knees and tightened himself into a ball. The durasteel walls of the canister were cold. She slid the top on, leaving a crevice for him to breathe.

"Here we go."

She started the repulsorlift motor, and Trever felt the hum come up through the bottom of the canister. He felt himself move, felt every turn of the hallway.

Then something changed — the light, the noise — and he knew he was in the hangar.

"Leaving this for disposal," the woman said. "Class D, toxic, so not to be opened."

"Affirmative." The clipped, mechanical-sounding voice of a stormtrooper.

And then the lid was slid back. He looked up into lovely dark eyes.

"This will be loaded onto a gravsled and taken back to the battalion. It's done by droids, so wait until they're busy negotiating air traffic. Just be sure and get off before it goes to the garrison. Good luck, whoever you are."

"Wait." He put his hand up to stop the canister lid from sliding back. "You've planned this already. This was your escape route."

She bit her lip. "Yes."

"But once I do it, you won't be able to take it."

She met his gaze for a long moment. He saw that she was giving up something that kept her going, gave her a reason to hope. If things became too bad, she would always be able to escape. Now she had no hope.

"Just go," she said, and closed the lid.

He rested his cheek against the cool metal. He felt no fear. He was ready for whatever came. He was so tired of running.

Soon he was lifted and smashed down again. He felt the lurch of the gravsled as it moved.

He waited until he heard the sounds of heavy

air traffic, pedestrians, the city of Ussa coming to life. Even without being able to see, he was able to track their progress through the city just by listening for familiar sounds. He waited until he was certain they were in the center of the city, the most populous district of Bluestone, and then he eased open the lid. The droids were simple service droids, but they had blasters built into their trunks. Now they were busy monitoring air traffic and controlling the gravsled. He wiggled out of the canister. A passing airspeeder pilot noted him, but this was Bellassa, where every citizen kept his or her mouth shut, so he looked away.

Crouching behind the canister, Trever waited for the next traffic stop. Then he leaped off the gravsled. It was about eight meters to the ground, and he hit hard, feeling the shock in his knees. But he rolled and stood up quickly.

He lost himself in the surging crowd. The sounds of the city were familiar and comforted him. He made his way to the safe house. As he drew near, his steps dragged. He didn't want to break the news. He didn't want to say it out loud.

Wil opened the door. He grabbed Trever by the elbows and pulled him inside. "What happened? Where's Amie?"

"Captured."

Wil sagged against the wall. "I've been up all night . . . waiting. Roan?"

"Ferus was captured, too. Vader was there."

Slowly, Wil straightened. "Roan."

"Dead." Trever felt his mouth twist out of shape.

He heard a moan, and Dona entered, her hands against her mouth.

Wil, who was always so strong, shocked Trever by simply lowering himself to the hallway floor. He put his head in his hands.

Wil had always been so brusque and remote. He was a legendary figure in Ussa, one of the founding members of the Eleven. Trever had never known that he could be overcome like this. It added to his own fear, and he started to shake again.

Dona put her strong hand on his shoulder. "Come on."

He followed her into the house. She pushed him down on a sleep couch and covered him with two blankets. "You need to get warm."

Trever realized how cold he was.

She disappeared and came back with a mug of scalding tea. "Drink this."

"I can't."

Wil appeared. He crossed the room and crouched down next to him. "It happens sometimes after a battle. The shaking. You'll be all right."

Trever hid his face from Wil.

"It's happened to me," Wil said. "More than once. So don't be ashamed."

Wil disappeared again. Trever drank the tea, not tasting it, just feeling the warmth spread out through his bones.

It seemed to take a long while before Wil reappeared.

"It's on the HoloNet now. They're bragging about it." Wil looked as though he'd aged ten years in the past half hour.

"I saw Roan die," Trever said. "Vader acted so fast. No one expected it. Roan didn't even have a blaster in his hand —" He saw anguish mirrored in Wil's eyes.

Roan had tossed him bakery rolls for breakfast and advice when he needed it. He'd let him sleep in the office when it was cold and looked the other way if Trever lifted a few credits on his way out the door. And then, when Trever was no longer a petty thief but a fellow resistance fighter, he had never made him feel less than anybody else. He had accepted him. Together with Ferus, he was the closest to family that Trever had known since his own family had died, every last one of them. Mother. Father. Brother. Roan.

He reached into his tunic to the pocket that lay against his skin. He pulled out the chip and handed it to Wil. "There's something on it. Something they were able to discover."

Wil took it. "At least we have this."

Trever looked up. He could feel something clenched inside him, something unfamiliar, and he realized it was fear that had dug in, that might never leave. "Wil," he whispered, "for the first time . . . I think we might lose."

Wil's hand tightened on him. "We won't lose. But I have to get you off-planet."

Trever straightened. "No!"

"I contacted Flame. You're both going to Coruscant."

"I want to help here!"

"You can't, Trever. It's only a matter of time before they start looking for you, too. They've traced the vehicle that you and Amie and Roan took to the factory, and they know you were part of the group. There was a hidden security cam at a checkpoint. Flame has volunteered to get you off-planet, and Dexter Jettster has agreed to allow both of you to enter his safe house on Coruscant. You have friends there who are waiting for you."

Trever looked from Wil to Dona. What they weren't saying, but what he knew, was that if he insisted on remaining, he would endanger all of them. He had to find the courage not to stay but to leave.

He rarely thought about whether he was brave. He had bounced from one situation to another and held himself together more out of stubbornness than anything else. Courage didn't live in him, the way it had lived in Roan. Trever knew now that he had never been brave before, only ignorant. Despite the battles he'd seen, the things he'd witnessed, he'd never truly realized what he was up against until last night.

He couldn't find his courage. He just had to accept his fear. And keep on going.

He nodded his agreement. In his heart he said his first good-bye to Roan. He knew that letting go of Roan would be done by centimeters, a small bit at a time.

But he did not say good-bye to Ferus. He would see him again. If he let go of that hope, he would let go of too much.

During the flight to Coruscant, Flame let him be, allowing a comfortable silence that gave him room to sleep and try to eat and gather himself for whatever came next. Dex had arranged a landing site for her, and she concealed the ship in a hangar that held many battered, and no doubt unregistered, vehicles.

"Coruscant is finding ways to get around the Empire," Trever said, looking around.

"It's inevitable," Flame said. "Even a powerful government can't patrol every centimeter of space." She turned to him. "We find the places they can't get to, and we hide there."

Trever thought of the asteroid base. A tiny wisp of hope, as ghostly as smoke, twined through him. He climbed out of the starship and trailed behind Flame as she strode toward the turbolift.

They descended to the Orange District. Trever remembered the way. He never forgot a route. He led the way now, through the twisting amber-toned streets, to the alley full of switchbacks and dead ends that led to Dex's safe house.

They walked into chaos. Astri stood, straining to get around Oryon, who was blocking the door with his large frame. Keets sat on the steps, his head in his hands. Curran, his shoulder bandaged, leaned against the wall. And Dex in a repulsorlift chair, floated nearby, his four hands gesticulating, one pair clasped, the other waving.

"Astri, we can help you if you let us," Dex was saying. "We need a plan."

"I can do it myself. We're wasting time!" Astri stamped her boot. "With every second you're holding me back, they're taking him away! He could be off-planet at any moment, he could be anywhere!"

"What happened to Lune?" Trever asked, stricken. No one answered him.

"We know where he is." Curran's voice was soft. "That's what we're trying to tell you."

"Where is he?" Astri wheeled to confront him.

"We need a plan," Oryon repeated. "You can't go there and —"

"Where is he?" Astri screamed.

"He's been taken to the Imperial Naval Academy," Dex said. "He's been enrolled."

"Bog," Astri said bitterly. "I knew he was behind this; I just didn't think he could have the wits to pull it off."

"He didn't need wits, he needed resources," Clive said. "He has that now. Sano Sauro is in charge of the academy. It's a demotion for him, but Bog and Sauro are allies from way back, as you know."

"You can't go running there by yourself," Dex said. "There's high security all around it. Even parents can't get in if they don't have clearance. And you *won't* have clearance."

"So what's your great plan?" Astri asked, a challenge in her voice. Her chin lifted, and her eyes flashed her defiance. Trever could see she didn't trust anyone to go after Lune but herself.

The others exchanged glances. "Well, we don't have one yet," Oryon admitted. "We just discovered where he was a few minutes ago."

"Astri, my lovely, you've got to trust us," Clive said. "Such as we are. Look around. We have plenty of skills here. We'll figure it out. We'll get him back. All of us."

Keet's voice was hoarse. "It's a promise. I'll die trying, but I'll get him back to you."

"I don't need promises. I need to go. I have to go get him." Astri's eyes filled with tears. "You think he's so strong, and he is. But he's still a boy. He can still be afraid. I have to try, I'll say I'm his mother, I'll demand —"

"That's just what Bog wants you to do," Oryon said firmly. "If you show up, you'll be arrested in the time it takes you to walk up the ramp."

Astri's body suddenly collapsed in on itself, and she folded herself in two, crouching near the floor, her forehead against her clenched hands.

Everyone began to talk at once, about the academy's location, probable security, where to procure a getaway vehicle, if the delivery services would be vulnerable to infiltration.

Trever stepped forward. "I have a plan," he said.

Everyone stopped talking. Everyone looked at him.

"I'll enlist," he said.

CHAPTER TWENTY-ONE

Again and again Ferus relived the moment when the lightsaber went through Roan's body. Again and again he felt the shock of it. Again and again he wondered if he could have moved, if he could have foreseen it, if he hadn't been so stupid, so slow, so convinced that Darth Vader would follow procedure, instead of striking out at a man who held no weapon against him.

He was in a cell, alone. He lay on the hard ferrocrete floor, his cheek against it. He knew why Vader had let him keep his lightsaber. It was a taunt. Vader knew it would torture Ferus to feel its familiar weight on his belt, to put his fingers on its handle, and know that his training had meant nothing. His lightsaber was useless. Vader was right.

Somewhere above him was sky and space and countless stars, and he was just a particle in the galaxy, and he was alone. Roan was gone. Their friendship had been full of separations, but they had always found each other again. They had trusted each other and watched each other's backs, and in one moment of criminally stupid miscalculation he had underestimated his opponent, and because of that, Roan was dead.

Because of him.

Life would go on around him, but he wouldn't be the same. He turned a different face to the galaxy now. The grief had changed him forever. He felt that as clearly as he could feel the ferrocrete against his cheek.

Roan's death had introduced fear to his life. His powers were so puny compared to what he faced. His will had carried him through. Now he realized that in the most secret recesses of his heart, he had held out one hope. That one day this would be over and he could go back to his life with Roan. He hadn't known the meaning of family when he'd been with the Jedi, but now he did, and the loss of it was impossible to bear.

Which proved he wasn't a Jedi. Attachment shouldn't be his reason for going on.

If he wasn't a Jedi, what was he?

And what did it matter? For soon he'd be dead. How curious to feel that he wouldn't mind.

But before they killed him, he would replay Roan's death again and again.

The lightsaber moved so fast, it was as though it jumped from Vader's hand. The mortal strike was assured and driven by the Force, the dark side that surrounded Vader and pulsed steadily from him. He had only been a blur.

Ferus suddenly sat up. He had heard a voice as clearly as if it had been spoken aloud.

Break it down, Ferus.

Obi-Wan? That was what he would say, in that cool way that could be so annoying.

Break down the movement; don't see it as a blur. You're a Jedi — yes, you are! — so be a Jedi.

He didn't feel like a Jedi. But he would obey that voice and try to break it down.

He closed his eyes and grabbed the memory. This time he struggled to leave his feelings behind. He had to see it clear.

He saw Darth Vader move now. He saw the curl of his cape. The way he turned his body, the position of his feet, the way his arm moved. He had used a classic Jedi shun move, rotating the lightsaber 360 degrees, but the rotation had moved so fast he'd been unable to track it.

Break it down.

Form IV. Then Form VII, the most advanced Jedi form. Done aggressively, with impeccable control.

Coldness gripped his heart. Jedi moves.

The movement had been done with a grace and finesse that rendered it not part of a drill but part of Vader's body. He brought an individual flair to it that made it his own.

Something familiar about that form. An aggression, a confidence . . . It struck a memory he couldn't touch. *But who could it be?*

If he could only know how old Vader was. Had he been on the Council? Such expertise suggested it.

I know him. I know the way he moves.

But everyone he'd studied with was dead. He couldn't say for certain that every Jedi he'd ever met was dead, but he knew the fate of all the Padawans. It had to have been an instructor, or perhaps a Jedi Master who had been away for long periods, so long he had lost his connection to the Jedi Temple, and Palpatine had exploited it. . . .

How could a Jedi be turned? It didn't seem possible, not to any Jedi he had personally known.

His door hissed open. Emperor Palpatine himself stood in the doorway, flanked by Red Guards.

Ferus rose to his feet.

Palpatine swept in, his hands hidden in the folds of his robes. The guards stayed outside as the door hissed closed.

"I am considering your fate," he said.

Ferus didn't react. He waited for the trap.

"It was a regrettable incident. Apparently you noted the security breach — although you lied about my asking you to monitor security. Perhaps we can accept that you were zealous in your desire to impress me — and unfortunately those who broke in were known to you.

Naturally, Lord Vader believes that you were part of the mission, and I must say, in a contest between his word and yours he will win."

Ferus wondered what Palpatine was getting to.

"And the fact that you took arms against Lord Vader is, of course, grounds for execution in itself. Yet."

Palpatine walked a few steps closer. Ferus wished he wouldn't. The air around him was so foul.

"I will confide in you that lately I feel that Lord Vader has been overreaching his authority. The killing of Roan Lands, for example. Very bad. We are in the midst of a delicate operation here on Bellassa. We want the support of the people. Support for the resistance was weakening, and now it will be inflamed again. Very unfortunate. It is my task to achieve stability in the galaxy. This means I am allowed to break the rules. The rules, for example, about punishment for attacking an Imperial high officer."

Ferus still didn't speak. He would let this play out. He had no interest in what Palpatine would say. He was done playing this game.

"If only I had someone I could really trust," Palpatine said. "Someone who understood my goals. If I found that someone, the gifts I could give him would be . . . immense."

Ferus looked away. He wished Palpatine would stop talking.

"The power over life and death," Palpatine said.

Ferus didn't turn, but he felt the hairs on the back of his neck rise.

"Ah, I see I have your full attention at last. I can teach you things that will make you more powerful than Vader. It will take time. But only time."

More powerful than Vader. Was it possible?

"Yes, it is possible," Palpatine said. "For I created him, did I not?" He took another small step toward Ferus. This time Ferus didn't shrink back.

"You have the potential to be the greatest Jedi ever known," Palpatine hissed. "You have all the raw materials. You only lack training. You will be able to use the Force in ways you never dreamed of."

Palpatine paused, letting his words hang in the air.

"Too much to grasp, is it? Let us take it step-by-step, then. First, I will put the Inquisitors at your disposal. Senator Sano Sauro has a plan to gather Force-adepts. Lord Vader isn't interested in this, but it has possibilities. But *you* could take over the search for the Force-adepts. With the help of Inquisitors. Sauro is getting nowhere because he doesn't understand the Force. It takes a Force-adept to find one."

He could do this. He could gather the Force-adepts, and instead of turning them over, he could bring them to the asteroid.

And all the while he would be growing more powerful. Until he could challenge Lord Vader himself.

This time he would not find himself hanging in the air like a useless, boneless thing, at Vader's mercy.

This time he would be the one to surprise Vader. Vader would be the helpless one. And Roan would be avenged.

Vader had made him a broken man, but he could be put back together.

He met Palpatine's gaze for the first time. He looked into the dark pits of his eyes.

"I'm ready to learn," he said.